"Under the circumstances, I thought it was best to show up here unannounced."

"Circumstances? What circumstances?" Cameron asked, his mouth twisted. He let out a brittle laugh. "Are you talking about the fact that your father nearly bankrupted this town and then fled like a thief in the night? Or the fact that you're not exactly welcome in this town?"

"All of that I suppose," she said in a soft voice. "I knew if I had called beforehand, you would have refused to see me. Maybe even run me out of town again."

His eyes cut straight through her. "You're right. I would have told you to stay away. For good." He spoke through gritted teeth. It seemed as if he was on the verge of exploding.

Even after all this time, it wounded her to see so much animosity in his beautiful green eyes.

Cameron's harsh voice cut into the silence. His eyes sparked [...] brought you back [...] So, let's cut to the [...] here?"

D1020375

Belle Calhoune grew up in a small town in Massachusetts. Married to her college sweetheart, she is raising two lovely daughters in Connecticut. A dog lover, she has one mini poodle and a chocolate Lab. Writing for the Love Inspired line is a dream come true. Working at home in her pajamas is one of the best perks of the job. Belle enjoys summers in Cape Cod, traveling and reading.

Books by Belle Calhoune

Love Inspired

Reunited with the Sheriff
Forever Her Hero
Heart of a Soldier
An Alaskan Wedding
Alaskan Reunion

Alaskan Reunion

Belle Calhoune

HARLEQUIN® LOVE INSPIRED®

Recycling programs
for this product may
not exist in your area.

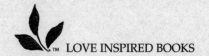

LOVE INSPIRED BOOKS

ISBN-13: 978-0-373-71944-0

Alaskan Reunion

www.Harlequin.com

Printed in U.S.A.

Where you go I will go,
and where you stay I will stay.
—*Ruth* 1:16

For my brother, David.
You're the bravest hero I know.

Acknowledgments

For all the readers who have embraced
this Alaska series and who have let me know
that they are waiting for more stories.

For my editor, Emily Rodmell, for being
so enthusiastic about Love, Alaska.

Thanks to my fellow Love Inspired authors
Sarah Varland and Angel Moore. Sarah—
thanks for allowing me to constantly pick your
brain about life in Alaska. Angel—thanks for all
the pictures, cool facts and Alaska inspiration.

Chapter One

"It's too late to turn back now," Paige Reynolds muttered, her steps slowing as she neared her destination. Snow gracefully fluttered down from the pewter sky in Love, Alaska. She stuck her tongue out and tried to catch a snowflake. April weather in Alaska was unpredictable to say the least. Snow one moment and then nothing but blue skies the next. It was so cold she could see her breath swirling in the air right in front of her face.

From this vantage point, Jarvis Street looked quaint enough to be featured on an old-fashioned postcard. She, of all people, knew better than to give in to sentimentality. Greeting her past head-on wasn't going to be a pleasant experience. Not by a long shot.

She'd stuffed her honey-blond hair under her hat and ducked her head down in order to minimize the possibility of being recognized by any of the townsfolk. Her arrival yesterday by seaplane just as it was getting dark had been deliberate. Landing in Love just as the sun went down lessened the chances of anyone noticing her.

Love, Alaska, a small fishing village, was located off the Pacific Ocean, on the southeastern tip of the state. She'd flown into Anchorage from her home in Seattle before taking the short flight to Love. She could only imagine the villagers' reaction if they'd stumbled upon the secret she was cradling in her arms as she stepped off the plane. Paige had known from having lived in this town for years that few people would be hanging out at the pier at sunset. It was very unlikely that any of the villagers would have pulled out the welcome mat for her even if they had known of her return.

If anyone had told her a year ago that she'd ever come back, she would have called them crazy. The locals had run her out of town almost two years ago in the wake of a financial scandal involving her father, the town of Love's treasury and the man who had once owned her heart. Even though she'd had no knowledge of her father's embezzlement, she'd been caught in the cross fire and regarded as guilty by association. The daughter of Robert Reynolds had been deemed unwelcome in the town she had always adored. That knowledge still burned inside her.

It was a little bit ironic, considering all the media reports she'd seen recently about young women flocking to the town due to Mayor Jasper Prescott's Operation Love campaign. Because of the female shortage in town, Jasper had reached out to the media and given an interview in which he invited eligible women to come to Love in order to be matched up with the single men.

She was probably the only woman the town wouldn't welcome with open arms.

It was all right. They didn't need to greet her with

a ticker-tape parade. What mattered most was that she was back, with an agenda that might be beneficial for everyone in town, if they would only listen to her. She bit her lip as a rising tide of anxiety rose up inside her. There was no telling what might happen once the villagers discovered she had returned. As far as they were concerned, the treachery of Robert Reynolds had cost them a cannery deal that would have greatly improved the financial status of their town.

The fishing village of Love had always been abundant in cod, salmon, pollock and halibut. The idea to build a cannery had been an excellent one. It would have created jobs for hundreds of residents, increased local revenue and put the town on the map with regards to the export of canned salmon. It had also been the hope that people would move to Love as jobs became available.

Her father's greed and selfishness in stealing the money earmarked for the venture had put a stop to those dreams and wounded a lot of people. And it had led to the town's financial downturn when creditors sought payment for construction of the cannery. Trying to help repair the damage to the town would hopefully lead to her own personal healing. Despite her father's treachery, she wanted to uphold his dying wish of redemption. And she needed to introduce her baby daughter to a father who had no idea about her existence. After all this time, she needed to do the right thing.

Everyone deserved forgiveness and an opportunity to make amends. But now being back in Love made her question whether her goals were way out of her reach. Had the choice to return to Alaska been a wise one?

Lord, please let this decision be the right one. My beautiful Emma needs to know her dad and he has a right to know her. And I need to make amends for my father's actions and repair some of the damage he inflicted. I want to be a source of healing for all the villagers. And, if possible, I want to provide redemption for my father. So much is riding on this!

Paige felt the corners of her mouth tilting upward into a smile as the wooden sign embossed with gold came into view. The Moose Café. Cameron Prescott's establishment. Her ex-boyfriend. The only man she had ever loved. Her knees trembled underneath her, threatening to give way at any moment. She steadied herself against the sheer magnitude of what the sign meant. Her father's treachery hadn't broken Cameron. He'd picked himself up, dusted himself off and built this café out of nothing but pure will and determination. That was who he was at his very core. She was so proud of him she could almost burst.

Cameron had been the love of her life. She'd long ago come to terms with the fact that he always would be. She had known he was special the very first time she'd laid eyes on him as a shy preteen. Since she and her parents had lived in Seattle for most of the year, she'd been able to catch only random glimpses of Cameron during summer vacations or holiday trips. Everything had changed with her mother's untimely death, her father's early retirement and their relocation to Alaska when she was fifteen. With Hazel Tookes, beloved owner of the Black Bear Cabins, playing matchmaker, she and Cameron had started dating and became a couple when they were seventeen. They had taken a break in their relationship when Paige had left Alaska to attend college. Upon her return four years later, they had picked up right where they had left off. Everything had been wonderful between them until the bottom fell out of their world.

Tears pricked her eyes at the thought of all Cameron had endured since the cannery deal fell through. The town had trusted him, along with her father, to deal with all aspects of getting the business up and running. They'd been in charge of hiring the employees, getting additional funding, overseeing the construction of the factory and handling the funds the town had appropriated toward the endeavor. When her father absconded with the town's money, the whole project had folded. And Cameron had been branded as an incompetent fool. Everyone had whispered about how he had let the wool be pulled over his eyes by a con man.

Even after all this time, the guilt threatened to pull her under. Her father's actions had torpedoed Cameron's life and created ripples throughout Love. She pushed past the painful emotions, knowing she had to keep moving forward. She'd come too far to lose her nerve now. Even though she'd made mistakes along the way, the time had come to bridge the gap between them. It was time to lay everything on the table.

Paige peered into the huge bay window, basking in the soft glow emanating from inside. The café had a rustic charm. A quick glance reassured her that all the customers were gone. A black-and-white Closed sign hung on the door. Her pulse quickened as a familiar sight came into view. Hazel was vigorously cleaning off a table. With her commanding height and silver hair, the older woman had a striking appearance. She was one of the most formidable women Paige had ever known.

Gruff, loyal Hazel. She had a tough exterior but a marshmallow center. Once, not too long ago, they'd been friends.

Paige turned the knob and, meeting no resistance, pushed open the door and stepped inside. The little bell over the frame jangled. Warmth enveloped her like a welcoming hug. The savory smell of coffee wafted in the air. The aroma of baked bread rose to her nostrils. She inhaled deeply, then exhaled. The door made a clicking sound as she shut it behind her, leaving the snow and the cold in her wake. She took her woolen hat off her head and shook it free of snow, then quickly peeled off her mittens. Paige ran her fingers through her hair and smoothed a few flyaway strands back in place. Her heart thundered inside her chest.

"Sorry. We're closed for the day. Stop by tomorrow morning and I'll make you the best waffles known to man. I'll even throw in a mochaccino on the house." Hazel's voice rang out loud and clear. It had an unmistakably brusque quality. She continued to focus on cleaning the table without even bothering to look up. After stacking a few plates and cups on a tray, she picked it up and balanced it against her middle.

"Hello, Hazel." Paige's simple greeting caused the older woman to swing her head up and lock gazes with her from across the room. A high-pitched squeak slipped past Hazel's lips. The tray slipped from her hands, landing with a loud crash on the hardwood floor. Liquid spewed everywhere. Hazel stood there like a statue with her mouth agape.

"Hazel! Are you okay? What happened? What's wrong?" Cameron's voice washed over her like a welcome rain after months of drought.

He came rushing from the other room to Hazel's side, and for a few seconds Paige was able to gaze at him without his being aware of her scrutiny. She clenched her hands at her sides as a rising tide of emotion overtook her in powerful waves. He was still achingly handsome. His chocolate-brown hair had grown out a little so that it now hung a bit past his ears. His profile was strong and manly. Paige couldn't see his eyes, but she knew the moment they connected with hers she would have to steady herself against the impact.

He was wearing a dark brown, long-sleeved T-shirt with a cartoon moose on it. In other circumstances it would have made her laugh out loud.

She soaked in as many details as she could in a matter of seconds. She wanted to savor the visual he was giving her.

A strong desire to burrow herself against his chest swept over her. His strong arms had always provided protection. And love. It had been a long time since she had experienced that type of comfort and closeness. She stuffed down the urge to reach for him. Those days were long gone.

"Cameron." Hazel uttered his name and then jutted her chin in Paige's direction. With a look of confusion etched on his face, he swung his gaze in her direction.

Time slowed down, and for a moment it felt as if it were only the two of them standing in the room. Everything else just faded away.

Cameron's green-hazel eyes flickered, and she watched as a half-dozen emotions ran across his face. He took a step forward, then stopped. Hazel grabbed hold of his T-shirt sleeve and pulled him back to her side. She was in full Mama Bear mode.

"What are you doing here?" Cameron asked in a curt voice. His expression was now shuttered.

"Hello, Cameron," she said with a nod in his direction. "I—I'm sorry to just drop in like this, but under the circumstances, I thought it was best to show up here unannounced."

"Circumstances? What circumstances?" Cameron asked, his mouth twisted. His eyes seemed dazed. He let out a brittle laugh. "Are you talking about the fact that your father nearly bankrupted this town and then fled like a thief in the night? Or the fact that you're not exactly welcome here?"

"All of that, I suppose," she said in a soft voice. "I knew if I had called beforehand, you would have refused to see me. Maybe even run me out of town again."

His almond-shaped eyes cut straight through her. "You're right. I would have told you to stay away. For good." He spoke through gritted teeth. It seemed as if he was on the verge of exploding.

Her mouth was as dry as sandpaper. She felt as if she'd lost all her nerve under the heat of Cameron's anger. And Hazel was glaring at her with such venom. Her harsh facade served a purpose. She was protecting Cameron, who was the closest thing she had to a son. It warmed her to know that she was still looking out for him.

"Hazel, would you give us a minute? Alone?" It took every ounce of courage she had to make the request. Hazel had been shooting daggers at her ever since she'd walked in.

The older woman's eyes bulged and her frown grew even more ominous.

"If you think I'm leaving Cameron here alone with you so you can torture him some more—" Hazel blustered.

"It's fine, Hazel," Cameron interrupted. He placed an arm around her shoulders and gave her a squeeze. "Thanks for the backup, but I'll be all right."

A silent form of communication passed between them. With a quick nod at Cameron, Hazel strode off toward the back of the café, her heavy footsteps the only sound echoing in the room.

Though she had asked for a private moment with Cameron, a feeling of awkwardness settled over her. An obvious tension hummed in the air between them. The intensity blazing from his eyes made her look away from him. Even after all this time, it wounded her to see so much animosity in his beautiful green-hazel eyes. She wrapped her arms around her middle. Her gaze focused on the coffee pooling on the floor and the shards of the shattered mugs that needed to be cleaned up.

Cameron's harsh voice cut into the silence. His eyes sparked like molten fire. "Whatever brought you back to Love has to be huge. So, let's cut to the chase. What are you doing here?"

* * *

Paige's mouth opened, then closed. She cleared her throat. He easily recognized the signs of her anxiety. Her warm hazel eyes blinked rapidly. She bit her lip, shifting from one foot to another. Time hadn't lessened her impact. As always, she took his breath away with her beauty. Her golden hair fell all around her shoulders in waves. He couldn't help but appreciate her stunning features and heart-shaped face. She was the most beautiful woman he'd ever known. But unlike how he had in the past, he wasn't about to tumble over the edge. Been there, done that. Falling for her had cost him everything. He had nothing more to give her.

Now when he looked at Paige Reynolds, all he saw were flashing warning signs.

"I'll ask you again. What are you doing here?" He repeated the question, his tone curt. "It's pretty foolish to come back to the scene of the crime."

She winced. Her eyes flickered with emotion. "I have some unfinished business here in town," she said. "Some things I need to settle up."

Bitter laughter burst from deep inside him. His lips curved into a sneer. "Business? The last business you conducted in this town left Love on the verge of bankruptcy. Let me warn you, our coffers are empty, if you're hoping for a repeat performance."

She visibly bristled. Anger flared in her eyes. "That wasn't my doing, Cameron. I've said it before and I'll say it again. I had no idea what my father was up to when he was working on the cannery deal with you."

"Right," he snapped. "Tell me another one, only this

time please realize that I'm not the same fool I was two years ago."

"I never thought you were," Paige said in a soft voice that brought him back to a point in time when she'd been his everything. His stomach twisted painfully. Seeing her after so long made him feel as if he'd been sucker punched in the gut. That was what it felt like to be staring into Paige's big, expressive eyes. The pain rippling through him served as proof that he wasn't over the past. Not by a long shot. The weight of it was sitting on his chest like a five-hundred-pound elephant.

"But I was a fool," he said in a low tone that matched her own. "A complete and utter fool to let my heart rule my head."

She shook her head, the long strands of her hair swirling about her face. "I want to make things right, Cameron. My father regretted what he did. Believe it or not, that's the truth. That's why I'm here. I want to return some of the money my father stole. And I want to do whatever I can to help get the cannery up and running."

Paige's words nearly knocked him off his feet. She was here to revive the project? And give back some of the money her father had stolen? That was crazy!

"You're about two years too late to resurrect the cannery deal, although I'm not about to say no to a big fat check made out to the town of Love," he spit out. The old resentment was rising up in him again. Try as he might, he couldn't contain his emotions. They were bubbling over like an overflowing pot on a stove.

She took a few steps toward him, quickly swallowing up the space between them. Her nearness made him want to take a step backward. Having her so close was dangerous to his equilibrium. His fingers itched to reach out and tuck a few strands of her glossy hair behind her ear. Or run his palm against her cheek. He shook his head to rid himself of those treacherous notions. How could those thoughts have even crossed his mind?

"It's not too late. It can't be." Her voice rang out stridently. "This town still desperately needs the business."

"Those dreams died, right around the time you and your father absconded with the funds." Paige's eyes pooled with tears. Her chin quivered. He could tell she was trying to act brave, even though she was failing miserably. He shouldn't care that he'd hurt her with his gibe, but he did care. Even after all this time and everything she'd done to him, he still hated to see her suffer. It caused a physical ache inside him.

"So where is he? Your father? Mr. Big Shot. Shouldn't he be here making this speech? Or is he too afraid he'll be put in jail and brought up on charges?"

Tears slid down Paige's face and she choked back a sob. Her graceful fingers wiped away the evidence of her sorrow. She bowed her head for a moment, then slowly raised it, her mournful eyes meeting his gaze.

"He's dead, Cameron. My father passed away two months ago of liver cancer."

Cameron felt as if someone had knocked him in the teeth. Robert Reynolds was dead. His former mentor. The man who'd betrayed his trust and made him a town pariah. Paige's beloved father. He didn't know how to explain it, but he felt a slight ache in his soul. They had once been close friends, or so he'd believed. The feeling of loss surprised him since all he'd felt toward Robert for the past few years was a hot, burning anger.

Paige, an only child, was now alone in the world, having lost her mother when she was a teenager. Before she'd shown up here today, he'd thought he was well past caring about her hurts, but the sight of her looking so wounded and grief-stricken tugged at his heartstrings. He knew that, with no family to speak of, she must have gone through the ordeal alone, with no one to share the burden. He steadied himself against the feelings of sympathy coursing through him, knowing it wasn't wise to make himself vulnerable to the one woman who knew how to bring him to his knees. He'd vowed to never go down that road again. He couldn't. His very survival depended on it.

She stuck out a wobbly chin. "I know you think he's a monster, but he had remorse for what he did. On his deathbed he made me promise to right his wrongs." She shrugged. "So you see, I don't have a choice. I need to fix everything he destroyed."

"Everything?" Cameron asked with a raised eyebrow. Robert's treachery hadn't harmed just the town of Love. Cameron's relationship with Paige had been a casualty of the town scandal. Nearly everyone in town had believed Paige was in on her father's scam. Even though it had killed him to think she was capable of such duplicity, he'd grown to believe in her guilt, as well. Nothing else had made sense. As a result, everything in his life had fallen apart. He had been at rock bottom trying to claw his way out of the abyss. He had emerged on the other side, but not without an abundance of scars.

"I'm aware some damage can't be undone, no matter how much I wish otherwise." Her simple statement was full of meaning. Once it would have meant the world to him to hear her speak of regret and making amends. Now, with so much standing between them, her words seemed hollow.

"You're absolutely right," he snapped. "Some things can't be fixed."

She let out a sigh. "I know you're still angry, Cameron. And you have every right to be. But if you would only hear me out, you'd realize that what I'm proposing is in the best interest of this town. You can't let anger and bitterness cloud your judgment."

He raised a hand and sliced it through the air. "There are no buts or what-ifs or maybe-sos in this situation. I lost everything because of what happened. When your father embezzled those funds, I was left holding the bag. All fingers were pointing at me. I lost every shred of credibility I had. You have no idea what it feels like to have an entire town turn against you."

Paige raised an eyebrow. "Don't I? I was run out of here because the same suspicions were leveled against me. And I was just as innocent as you were, Cameron. I know what it feels like to have everyone turn against me. Including the man I loved."

The man I loved. She had loved him. Of that he'd always been certain. And he'd loved her in return. Madly. Devotedly. With every fiber of his being. He had dreamed of one day making Paige his wife. Because of her, he'd wanted to become a better man. And even though he still dreamed of pledging forever to a soul mate, he had a hard time imagining ever feeling that way again about anyone. So many of his dreams had been wrapped up in Paige. And her betrayal had left him wounded.

Despite the fact that dozens of women had arrived in town to participate in Operation Love, he never allowed himself to imagine getting into a relationship with any of them. The idea of being that vulnerable again terrified him. The past still loomed over him like a dark cloud.

Had he made the right decision when he'd forced Paige's hand and told her to leave town? For so long he hadn't even second-guessed himself, but now, after hearing her heartfelt words, a sliver of doubt crept in. Why had he been so convinced of her guilt? What had made him so willing to turn his back on the woman he had adored?

"Cameron. I can't pull this off without you. Nobody in Love is going to want to listen to what I have to say. No one will work with me to make it happen. The dream this town once had of opening a cannery is still viable. I know we could make it work." Paige's cheeks were flushed and her voice vibrated enthusiasm.

"We?" His head was feeling fuzzy. Had he heard her correctly? She wanted him to team up with her?

"I need your support to rally the townsfolk." Her shoulders drooped and she let out a sigh. "As you know, I don't have a lot of credibility here. But I do have an MBA and several projects to my credit."

"What are you asking me to do? I have a business to run now." Cameron looked around at the café. It meant the world to him. Making a success out of it had given him the redemption he'd craved. It gave him respectability after the cannery fiasco. Finally, people in town weren't shaking their heads at him anymore. He'd won them all over with hard work and grit, convincing them to make the Moose Café a staple in town. No way! He was done stepping out on a limb and taking leaps of faith. Once bitten, twice shy.

"Sorry to burst your bubble, Paige, but this town closed the door on that pipe dream a long time ago."

She narrowed her gaze. "Really? I've been keeping tabs on Love for a while now, Cameron. I know it's still suffering financially."

"Things have been improving bit by bit. Don't believe everything you hear," he snapped. For some reason it annoyed him to no end that Paige knew how badly they'd continued to struggle. They may have fallen on hard times, but the industrious townsfolk in Love had banded together to try to reverse the town's fortunes. That single fact made him proud to be part of this community. The town was down at the moment but not out.

A low buzzing sound cut into the silence. Paige fished in her pocket and pulled out a cell phone. She knit her brows together and peered at the screen. Her eyes slightly widened. "I—I'm sorry. I have to go, Cameron."

"Seriously, Paige? You can't just show up here after all this time and drop a bombshell like this and take off," he protested.

Paige locked gazes with him. "There's a lot more I have to say. Things I should have said a long time ago.

And whether or not you approve or disapprove, I'm going to try and make amends for my father's crimes. It's the only way I can look at myself in the mirror in the weeks and months ahead."

There she was. The Paige he'd fallen in love with well before he'd ever had the courage to tell her how he felt. Obstinate. Opinionated. And now she was here in front of him, determined to right her father's wrongs. Which meant she'd be staying right here in Love to make amends. There was no point in his standing in her way. That slight edge to her voice indicated she meant business.

"I'll be in touch with you tomorrow." With a nod in his direction, she turned on her heel and began to quickly walk away. Once she reached the door, Paige turned around and met his gaze. "By the way, I'm really proud of what you've done here. The Moose Café is beautiful. Some dreams can't be denied, can they?"

Before he could even respond, the jingling of the door serenaded Paige as she sailed out the door and into the Alaskan night.

"What just happened?" he muttered as he stood in the middle of his establishment wondering if he should follow after her or just leave it alone for now. Like a true force of nature, she'd blown into his world and left him feeling as if he'd been caught in the path of an unexpected storm.

As soon as Paige turned off Jarvis Street onto Main Street, she let out a deeply held breath. She'd faced Cameron head-on without backing down. And she was still standing! It had turned out better than expected even though she hadn't achieved her main objective during her visit. He needed to know about Emma.

A tight knot had been forming in her stomach all day. For weeks and months she'd planned for this very moment. And somehow it had slipped through her fingers. That only served to heighten the anxiety she felt about the situation. Leaving the Moose Café without telling Cameron the most important reason for her return hadn't been her intention. The text message she'd received had interrupted them, and due to the pressing matter at hand, she'd had no choice but to table their discussion for another time.

Cameron, you're a father. How exactly did one just blurt that news out? No matter how many times she had practiced her speech in the mirror, it never came out sounding right. Tears gathered in her eyes. She'd been so wrong about so many things.

If she was being honest with herself, telling Cameron about Emma wasn't something she'd wanted to do with Hazel within earshot. In her heart she'd wanted to tell him in a private moment shared by just the two of them. And that moment hadn't presented itself.

Ever since her daughter had come into the world, Paige had made her the number one priority in her life. Now it was time to give Cameron that choice, as well.

As a woman who'd moved toward her faith after becoming a mother, she harbored regrets about not being married to Emma's father when her daughter was conceived. Her actions hadn't been consistent with her upbringing or her own moral compass. But in the aftermath of her dad's massive betrayal, she and Cameron had turned to each other for comfort. Days later she'd fallen under the town's suspicion and Cameron had distanced himself completely from her. With no other options, she'd left Love and headed back to Seattle. Her life had been in shambles until she'd made the discovery some weeks later that she was pregnant.

Looking back on her life, she realized that what had been missing had been a spiritual base. Even though she had always considered herself a joyful, content person, there hadn't been anything to anchor her to the world around her. Perhaps if her father had led a more spiritual life, he wouldn't have been so tempted by financial gain.

Bringing her beloved daughter into the world had given her life meaning. God had given her a foundation on which to stand. With His forgiveness, she had been able to move forward. Praying, attending church and being part of the faith community had all taken center stage. Because of Emma, her relationship with the Lord had strengthened and blossomed. For fourteen months Paige had lived every day with some measure of contentment—all the bitterness and anger she'd been harboring about the past had been soothed because of Emma and her faith.

But being back in Love meant facing up to her truths. Somehow she had to find a way to tell Cameron that he was the father of a baby girl.

Chapter Two

Cameron watched helplessly as Paige walked out of the Moose Café and hustled down the street at a fast clip. He drifted toward the window, his gaze trailing after her as she faded from sight. He pressed his eyes closed as the ache of loss swept through him.

Still, after all this time, it hurt to acknowledge that Paige was no longer a part of his life. Getting over her had almost killed him. Yet here she was, back in Love and vowing to make amends. Suddenly everything he'd been trying to forget had come bubbling back to the surface. Pain. Embarrassment. Loss. He didn't know what to do with all these chaotic feelings roiling around inside him. Even though he'd been trying to stuff down these raw emotions ever since he'd come face-to-face with Paige, they were still riding on the surface.

He couldn't help but wonder if he was being played again. Hadn't Paige mentioned returning a portion of the money her father had stolen? If that was true, it could help the community immensely. But he didn't want to get his hopes up without seeing an actual check in his hands made out to the town of Love, Alaska. He'd already been burned once by Paige and Robert Reynolds.

It was all coming at him too fast now—like an out-of-control train. He pulled out a chair and sank down in it, his shoulders slumped forward as he held his head in his hands. The sound of Hazel's clunky footsteps heralded her arrival. She bent down and began gathering up the ceramic pieces in a dustpan and wiping up the liquid on the hardwood floor.

She looked up at him. "Are you okay?" Her voice was filled with worry.

"Never better," he said. Hazel had already seen him at his worst. He couldn't count the number of times she'd consoled him when he'd broken down over Paige and the financial scandal that had sent shock waves through his hometown. There was no way he was going to burden her with any more of his misery.

She let out an indelicate snort. "You look like you've been run over by a truck."

Cameron shoved his hand through his hair and let out the breath he'd been holding. He stood up from his chair to face her. "I can't believe this is happening. Paige thinks she can undo the damage she and Robert caused. She thinks she can just stroll into town after all this time and put all the pieces back together."

"I heard every word she said," Hazel admitted, rolling her eyes. "She always did have a pie-in-the-sky mentality."

He frowned at her. "You were eavesdropping?"

Hazel planted her hands on her hips. "It's called watching out for me and mine. I saw the carnage she caused the first time around. I'm not about to let it happen again. Not on my watch!"

A sigh escaped his lips. "Hazel, I love you dearly, but I'm begging you to stay out of this. And whatever you do, please don't tell Jasper or Boone that she's back. I want a little time to digest everything before complete chaos breaks out."

Hazel quirked her mouth. A sinking feeling landed in the pit of his stomach.

Cameron folded his arms across his chest and narrowed his gaze. "Hazel," he said in a reproachful tone. "I hope you didn't—"

The door of the Moose Café burst open with a loud crashing sound. His brother Boone, town sheriff, and his grandfather, Mayor Jasper Prescott, came barreling into his establishment.

"Hey! Didn't you two read the sign? We're closed," Cameron shouted, knowing it was too late to stop the impending hurricane from whirling all around him.

Jasper darted his gaze around the café. "Where is she?"

Cameron crossed his arms again and rocked back on his heels.

"Who are you talking about?"

"You know who I'm talking about. That beautiful blonde trickster you were so enamored of for all those years. Miss Paige Reynolds. Daughter of the most crooked man who ever stepped foot into Love."

"Jasper! Knock it off! Let's keep the drama to a minimum," Boone barked. "Give him an opportunity to talk."

"I can't believe she had the nerve to come back here," Jasper fumed. "Returning like a bad penny!"

"Settle down, Jasper," Boone said, reaching out and clasping his hand around his arm.

He shrugged off his grandson's hand. "I won't settle down. As town mayor, I implore you to arrest her, Sheriff Prescott," Jasper said in a raised voice.

"There's no proof that Paige had anything to do with her father's scam," Boone explained. "We already went through this dozens of times. There's no grounds to charge her."

"There never was," Cameron said, a slight defensive edge to his voice.

Boone shot him a curious look. Cameron looked away from him. His older brother had a canny ability to see straight through him, right down to the things that mattered most. He couldn't afford that intense scrutiny right now, not when he was battling old feelings that were rising up in him like a strong tide.

"What about aiding and abetting a criminal? Rumor has it she reunited with that thieving dog once we ran her out of here. Doesn't that prove they were in cahoots?" Jasper asked.

Cameron shook his head at Hazel. "How long did it take you to call them? Two minutes?"

"I figured we might need a small army to run her out of town again," Hazel explained, her expression sheepish. "And they did need to know about her plans to give back the town's money."

"No one is getting rid of Paige," Boone said. "I'd like to talk to her about the funds she wants to return. That's important for Love's finances."

"And our future! This town needs money in the coffers," Jasper growled. "If you ask me, we should charge her interest."

Cameron rolled his eyes, resisting the impulse to show his grandfather the door. "Funny you should say that, since I don't remember asking you."

"So, Cameron. What did she say, exactly? How much is she giving the town? I must have missed that part," Hazel said.

"I don't know," Cameron mumbled, feeling foolish that he hadn't asked her for specifics. He'd been so blown away by her mere presence that he hadn't homed in on it. Was she really prepared to give a hefty sum of money?

"You didn't ask her?" Jasper shouted. He threw his hands up in the air and began muttering in a loud voice. "What a bunch of foolishness!"

"No, I didn't. I was pretty much blindsided when she strolled in here. It took a few minutes to get my thoughts together." Cameron ground out the words in a no-nonsense manner. It was just like Jasper to show up and start trying to boss him around. As long as they were in his place of business, he wasn't about to allow his grandfather to walk all over him.

"Stop being so insensitive," Hazel said in a loud stage whisper. "You're acting like a bull in a china shop."

Jasper and Hazel exchanged a long, meaningful look. Jasper's expression softened. He took a deep breath, then continued. "Well, if you beg my pardon for asking, where is she?"

Already Cameron was feeling weary. Normally, he could go a full twelve rounds with his grandfather, but he was still reeling from the unexpected encounter with his ex. He simply didn't have the strength at the moment. Paige's surprise appearance was resting heavily on his heart.

"There aren't too many places she could go, Cam. Matter of fact, there's really only one," Boone said, his dark brows knit together.

The homestead. The two-story log-cabin home and vast acreage that had belonged to the Reynolds family for generations. Years ago when Paige's father had been flush with money, he'd renovated the home and transformed it into a modern showcase. Although many villagers had wanted to seize the property after Robert's misdeeds came to light, homesteads in Alaska were not eligible for seizure.

And so it had sat unoccupied. Until now.

Three pairs of eyes were trained on him. It was clear what they wanted him to do.

"I'm not chasing after her. She said that she would talk to me more about all of this tomorrow." He shoved his hands in his front pockets.

"Ha! And you believe that?" Hazel cried out. "Fool me once, shame on me. Fool me twice, shame on you."

"Do you really want to leave all that in her hands instead of being proactive?" Boone asked. "This isn't personal, Cam. It's about the town. You need to find out if she's serious about the money. I wasn't going to mention it just yet, but we need an influx of cash in order to move forward with the production of Hazel's boots. This enterprise has become a lot more expensive than we anticipated. Strangely enough, Paige's return could be the answer to all our prayers."

Hazel had designed stylish and functional boots for the townsfolk that were now being mass-produced and sold throughout the United States in order to bring profit to the treasury's coffers. Boone's wife, Grace, had the brilliant idea to capitalize on the fashionable winter shoes as a way of boosting the local economy. For the first time in a long time, the residents of Love had hope of turning things around. But, like any new enterprise, it all boiled down to money.

The answer to all our prayers. Boone's words were ironic. Once upon a time he had believed that Paige was the answer to all his prayers. Only he'd been wrong. Although the love he'd felt for her had been stronger than anything he'd ever known, everything had come tumbling down like a stack of dominoes. He still felt as if he was picking up the pieces of his former life. Opening the Moose Café had been a huge step in the right direction. It had always been a dream of his to have his own establishment in his hometown. And even though people had lost faith in him, they'd come around once they'd got a taste of his unforgettable coffee drinks and sampled the delicious menu. Finally, his life was back on track.

And yet he still felt guilty about being fleeced by Robert Reynolds. He continued to struggle with his leading role in the town's financial downturn. Had he missed any warning signs along the way? Had his feelings for Paige blinded him to her father's larcenous nature? Those questions continued to plague him in the hours between darkness and dawn as he struggled to get some shut-eye on sleepless nights.

Was it possible that he could help make things right by working with Paige? The one thing he knew he was guilty of was being biased against anything she had to say. She'd burned him once before and he no longer trusted her. But in order to help the town, he might have to take a leap of faith and take her at her word. The very idea of it rocked him to his core.

"I'll do it," he said. "I'll go find Paige and get the information you want."

"That's more like it!" Jasper cried out. "I knew you'd come around."

Cameron reached for his coat and shrugged into it. He glared at his grandfather. "Don't get the impression I'm doing your bidding, Jasper. I'm acting in the best interests of this town. Considering my role in the economic downturn, it's the least I could do."

Boone approached him and placed his hand on his shoulder. "I know this isn't easy, Cam. I'm sure it stirs up a lot of memories. You want some company? I don't mind coming along for moral support."

He let out a sigh. "Thanks for asking, Boone, but I've got to handle this on my own. Go home to that beautiful wife of yours. I've got this."

His brother nodded in acknowledgment, his expression solemn.

Boone and his wife, Grace, were newlyweds. Despite

Grace having pretended to be a participant in Jasper's Operation Love campaign when she arrived in Alaska, she'd really been a journalist working undercover on a series about the town. In the end, their love had triumphed.

He couldn't even pretend to himself that he wasn't a little bit jealous of what Grace and Boone had together. It was what he had once believed he'd had with Paige. True, enduring love.

As he headed out the back entrance of the café and walked toward his red pickup truck parked in the lot, the full weight of the situation was sitting squarely on his chest. He'd once promised to never chase after Paige Reynolds again. And lo and behold, it was exactly what he found himself doing.

Paige navigated the darkened Alaskan roads like a semiprofessional driver. It was funny how the mind worked. She hadn't lived in this town for years, yet she could probably drive this road blindfolded. Some things a person never forgot. A tender word. The sweet verses to a song. Your baby's first cries. The only man you'd ever loved.

Coming face-to-face with Cameron had been an electrically charged, emotional moment. Her knees had been trembling the entire time. Not a day had gone by since she'd left Alaska that she hadn't thought of Cameron. His strength. The larger-than-life smile that almost took over his entire face. The sound of his laughter ringing out with such tremendous joy. The way he'd always looked at her with love shining from his eyes.

So much had changed since those wonderful days. Earlier, there had been nothing emanating from Cameron's eyes but disgust. And given everything at stake, it frightened her. Every night since Emma had been born, she'd prayed that his heart would soften toward her. Not for her sake but for Emma's. Clearly those prayers hadn't been answered. He'd been as implacable as granite.

She tightened her grip on the steering wheel. Once she had received the text message from Fiona, her nanny, she'd had no choice but to cut things short and head to the homestead. Emma needed her mother.

The sign heralding her arrival at The Last Frontier appeared just before she turned right into the long driveway and parked her loaner car in front of the house. After grabbing her purse and exiting the car, she climbed the front steps, silently admiring the wraparound porch and the rustic yet modern feel to the house. It seemed strange being here without her father. This house had been his pride and joy, back in the good old days before he'd lost his way.

Maybe she was being overly optimistic, but she was hoping it might feel like home again.

Before she could even put the key in the lock, Fiona Gersham pulled open the door and greeted her. She was holding Emma on her hip. With her round face, soothing voice and sweet expression, the middle-aged woman had given Paige a good feeling the moment she'd presented herself for the interview to be Emma's nanny. As her father's illness worsened, Fiona's presence in their lives had been a godsend. As much as her father had been vilified for his misdeeds, she'd never stopped loving him. And the grief that had consumed her after he'd passed away had been overwhelming. It had felt like being buried by an avalanche with no hope of rescue.

With God's love, Fiona's steady assistance and the almighty love she felt for Emma, she'd crawled her way out of the darkest days she'd ever known. She'd emerged ever changed. If losing Cameron and her father so close together hadn't broken her, nothing in this world ever would. Emma had come into her life like a bright light and given her a purpose. She'd been her rainbow after the storm.

Fiona stepped aside and ushered her out of the cold and into the toasty house. Emma held up her hands and gifted her with a beatific smile that traveled straight to her core.

"I'm so sorry to disrupt your meeting, Miss Paige. I tried to get her calmed down, but between the flight over here, the time difference and the new surroundings, I think the little lady is turned upside down."

She patted her nanny's shoulder. "It's okay, Fiona. You're right. It's been a long day for her." She scooped Emma up in her arms and cradled her against her chest. Smoothing her daughter's dark curls back, she pressed a kiss against her temple. "How's my sweet girl?"

"Want Mama. Night night." Emma's dark lashes were moist from crying. Paige's heart expanded by leaps and bounds every time she held her child in her arms. She wanted to give this precious little girl the world wrapped up with a big bow. Right now Emma needed her mother's loving arms and the comfort that only she could provide.

"Baba," Emma said, saying her word for *bottle*. "Me want baba."

Fiona made a face and handed Paige the bottle. "I've been trying to offer her this bottle for the last hour," she said with a low chuckle. "Guess she wanted her mother to feed her."

Mother. Just the sound of it rolling off Fiona's tongue gave her a feeling of elation. Motherhood was the most amazing role of her life. It was gratifying. Awe inspiring. Empowering. Being Emma's mother made her feel as if she could do anything. Climb the highest mountain. Rush into a burning building to save her child. Even return to a town whose citizens had falsely accused her and turned their collective back on her. Her daughter made her brave.

Paige gently rocked from side to side, knowing her daughter found it soothing. Emma reached up and tugged at her hair, then let out a high-pitched giggle. She jokingly shook a finger at Emma, resulting in another round of laughter. *Yes*, she thought with satisfaction. These were the simple moments that brought her joy.

A loud noise from outside drew her attention. It sounded like the crunching of a car's tires in the gravel driveway. Paige felt her entire body stiffening. Was someone outside?

"Miss Paige. I think someone just pulled up in the driveway," Fiona said as she turned and peered out the window.

Fear grabbed her by the throat. There were only two people in town who knew she was here. Cameron and Hazel. And for the life of her she couldn't imagine

Hazel taking the trouble to come all the way out here to the homestead. The sound of a car door slamming followed by footsteps caused a rush of adrenaline to course through her.

"Fiona, can you take Emma upstairs to her room? I'll be right up." She handed Emma over to Fiona, who made her way swiftly down the hall. On instinct, Paige turned off the light in the foyer, hoping that it might dissuade her visitor from knocking on the door.

Dear Lord, she prayed, *please make him go away. Please, please, please. Make him get back in his car and head back to town. This is way more than I can handle at the moment. I don't want Cameron to find out about his daughter like this.*

Cameron rapped on the door again, this time using a little more force. A light from inside had gone out while he was standing here on the front porch. He waited a few seconds, then knocked again. It wasn't even eight o'clock. Surely she hadn't turned in for the night.

"Open up, Paige. I know you're in here. I saw the lights from down the road and I know this house has been unoccupied since you left." He heard a rustling noise, then nothing further.

"I listened to what you had to say when you came by the café. Can't you give me the same courtesy?" he asked, trying to appeal to Paige's innate sense of fair play. Was she even the same person she used to be?

"It's late, Cameron. Can't we just talk tomorrow? It's been a long day." Her voice sounded slightly muffled from the other side of the door.

"I need to talk to you. Now. This can't wait till morning."

The click of a lock turning echoed in the stillness. The door crept open until he could see Paige standing there with her body blocking the entrance.

"I told you we could talk tomorrow," she said in a hushed tone.

He stepped forward. "Can I come in? There are some questions I need answers to."

Paige's hazel eyes were wide. Her complexion had lost a bit of its rosy color. "N-now isn't a good time, Cameron."

"And why is that? You showed up at my place of business unannounced and unloaded all this stuff on me, but I can't ask any follow-up questions?"

"You can," she said in a soft voice. "Just not now." She cast a quick glance over her shoulder.

Why was she looking behind her? Was someone staying at the house with her? All his nerve endings were suddenly on edge. Something about Paige's body language was sending out warning signals. She was hiding something from him.

"Mama!" The earsplitting cry came from inside the house. Paige's eyes began blinking rapidly and she took a step backward. She fumbled for a moment, then tried to shut the door. His arm snaked out, preventing her from closing it in his face.

"Mama?" His voice came out hoarse and ragged. The thought of Paige being a mother almost brought him to his knees. Had he failed to notice a wedding ring? Had Paige married someone else? Given birth to another man's child?

"I need to check on my daughter." Paige choked out the words. Cameron watched as she spun around and took a few steps toward an older woman who was standing in the foyer holding a wailing child. Feeling stunned, Cameron crossed the threshold and pushed the door closed behind him. The scene unfolding before his very eyes captivated him. He couldn't have looked away if he'd tried. Paige was tenderly cradling a toddler in her arms while the older woman muttered apologies. Within seconds the loud cries stopped. He heard a little chuckle burst forth from the baby. She had one of Paige's curls wrapped around her chubby finger.

"I'll put her down in a little bit, Fiona. Don't worry about us. Go get some rest."

"Thank you, Miss Paige. See you in the morning. Nighty night, sweet peach." The Fiona woman darted a curious glance in his direction, then headed up the stairs.

"Night night," the girl said, turning her head and waving her tiny hand at Fiona.

Cameron let out a gasp as he caught his first full-on glimpse of the little wailer. Nothing in his life up to this point had prepared him for this one moment in time. Everything around him stilled and hushed. With her chocolate-colored hair, wild curls and almond-shaped eyes, she evoked dozens of his own childhood photos. Her green-hazel eyes brought the truth home. He placed his fingers over the bridge of his nose and squeezed tightly, then blinked in rapid succession. Was he seeing things?

He might be all kinds of crazy, but in his humble opinion the toddler was his spitting image. Yes, indeed. This little girl was a Prescott, through and through.

Chapter Three

Paige could see the look of recognition as it passed over Cameron's face. Anyone with eyeballs could see the resemblance between Emma and her father. Although she'd always known Cameron to be a good man, she had no way of anticipating his reaction to this bombshell revelation. After all, she never would have believed that he'd have turned against her in the first place. She never could have predicted that their love story would disintegrate into ashes. The Cameron she'd been in love with had been loyal to a fault. And compassionate, as well as tender. Until he had stopped believing in her. Until he'd viewed her as a traitor.

Her body went rigid as she waited for him to speak, to say something about their baby girl. Little beads of moisture gathered on her forehead and she found herself swiping them away with the back of her hand.

"Is she mine?" Cameron asked in a guttural tone. His intense green eyes were focused on her like lasers.

"Yes," Paige acknowledged with a nod of her head. "She's yours."

His eyes held a dazed look. "Wh-when? H-how old is she?"

"I found out that I was pregnant right after I left Alaska. She's fourteen months."

Cameron shoved his hand through his dark mane. A slow hissing sound escaped his lips. His foot was tapping an unsteady rhythm on her hardwood floors. He began to clench and unclench his hands at his sides.

"You had my child and never said a word?" Anger rang out in his voice. His jaw clamped down and his expression darkened. "How is that possible?"

Paige tightened her grip on Emma, who was now frowning at Cameron. "We're not having this discussion in front of Emma. She's not used to loud voices."

"Emma. That's her name?" Cameron's voice had softened to something resembling tenderness. It catapulted her back to a place in time when they'd loved each other. Sometimes those days seemed so long ago it felt as if she'd dreamed them.

"Yes. After my mother," she said. "I still miss her every day, but it's my way of paying homage to her. She was a good woman. If I can be half the mother to Emma that she was to me—"

Emotion clogged her throat and she let her words trail off. Losing her mother in a car accident on an icy Seattle road at fourteen had changed the course of her life. The tragedy had left her and her father bereft for years. She had been the center of their home, and without her they'd floundered. Until they'd both decided to love each other as fiercely as she'd loved them. Her daughter's name would always remind her of grace and goodness and mercy. Each and every day, she prayed that Emma would be gifted with those attributes.

"It's a good name," Cameron conceded. "Your mother was an amazing woman. She had such a light about her. I always admired her quiet dignity and compassion."

Warmth filled her insides at the tender way he spoke about her mother. The feeling settled right inside her heart, providing her with much-needed comfort in this tense moment.

Emma let out a yawn and rubbed her eyes. She dropped her head onto Paige's shoulder. The warmth of her little body gave Paige a feeling of comfort.

"Cameron, I know there are probably a hundred things you want to say to me. Questions you need to ask. But I really need to put Emma down for the night. If I don't, she'll be a bear tomorrow."

He looked confused for a moment, as if he was still trying to make sense of this turn of events. "Can I watch you put her to bed? I won't say a word. I just want to see you put her to sleep."

Cameron's request surprised her. She'd figured that having just found out he was a father, he might need some time to process everything. She locked gazes with him, trying to gauge his thoughts. There was a look of such wonder in his eyes. He resembled an adorable little kid. And as always, she found it impossible to say no to him.

"Of course you can. Just walk softly. Her eyes are

already drooping," she whispered as she supported the back of Emma's head with her hand.

As Paige led the way upstairs, then toward the bedroom at the end of the hall, Cameron trailed behind her. He followed her almost soundlessly. Once she'd laid Emma down on the small twin bed, she began to rub her back and sing to her. It was the same song every night, the one her own mother had sung to her. Cameron stood off to the side, quietly taking it all in. His expression was thoughtful, reverent almost.

"Good night, little one," Paige crooned as she pulled the quilt over Emma's body and pressed a kiss to her cheek. She turned off the lamp sitting on the bedside table and made sure Emma's favorite night-light was lit up. Sleeping in a strange house might result in a middle-of-the-night awakening. If so, Paige would hear any cries or babbling on the baby monitor she'd placed nearby.

When she turned around to tiptoe out of the room, she noticed that Cameron was gone.

Watching Paige put their daughter to sleep had been a gut-wrenching experience for him. His daughter was achingly beautiful. And innocent. She'd looked so small and defenseless nestled up under her covers. A protective feeling had risen up inside him, one that shocked him by its ferocity. The earth-shattering knowledge that she belonged to him had ricocheted through him like a bullet. He knew from this moment forward he would fight all her battles and make sure everything was right in her world.

His little girl. He'd never imagined bringing a child into the world as a single, unmarried man. The dream had always been to stand at the altar and exchange vows with Paige before God and all their family and friends. It didn't sit well with him that the Cameron of two years ago hadn't been connected with his God or his faith. And he'd made mistakes in his relationship with Paige that he deeply regretted, although something told him he would never regret being a father to his precious little girl. He'd turned his life over to God two years ago when everything in his world had gone up in flames. His life was now firmly rooted in his faith with every step he took. Nothing could shake it.

And even though he harbored regrets about his poor choices, he knew that the Lord had a plan for him and sweet Emma.

Emma Prescott. He let out a groan. For all he knew, Paige had given her the last name of Reynolds. He let out a snort. That would go over like a lead balloon in this town.

How could something so delicate and wondrous and perfect have come from him? And how could Paige have hidden something so monumental? Hadn't she owed him the truth? *Lord, please help me make sense of this deception. I feel like I've been betrayed all over again.*

A myriad of emotions had flooded him when he'd watched Emma drift off into slumber. Joy. Wonder. And resting right on the surface…a righteous anger at Paige for keeping his daughter's existence a secret. Fury had been stoking inside him like a slow-burning fire. He'd left Emma's bedroom rather than run the risk of saying something negative to Paige in front of Emma. Try as he might to calm himself down, the questions continued to whirl all around him.

As he gazed out of the huge bay window in the living room, he found himself taking solace in the stunning vista that stretched out as far as the eye could see. The onyx sky was scattered with twinkling stars, while snow-dotted mountains loomed in the distance. If it had been light outside, he might even have been able to catch a glimpse of Deer Run Lake or Nottingham Woods.

Paige's footsteps echoed behind him. He turned around to face her, making sure to breathe in and out to calm himself. Tension crackled in the air between them.

She reached out and gently touched his arm, causing shivers of awareness to trickle straight through him. "Are you all right? I know everything must be coming at you like a freight train. Finding out you're a dad is going to take some getting used to, I imagine."

He ran a hand over his face. "I'm still in shock, I think," Cameron said. "I can't seem to wrap my head around the fact that I'm somebody's father."

Tears shimmered in Paige's eyes. "She's wonderful, Cam. I know I'm biased, but she'll wrap you right around her finger in no time at all."

Paige's words were tantamount to poking a grizzly with a stick. He didn't want to hear about how magnificent Emma was when he'd missed out on the first year of her life. He should have had the opportunity to experience it himself rather than hear it secondhand from Paige.

"I wish you'd—" He stopped himself, feeling frustrated by his inability to find the right words to express himself without finger-pointing or rage. He let out a strangled sound.

"Reached out to you and told you about Emma?" Paige asked in a low voice.

He frowned at her. "Why'd you do it? Was it some sort of payback for the town wanting to prosecute your father? Was it your turn to turn the tables on me because I wasn't in your corner?"

Paige shook her head. Her eyes narrowed. "None of those reasons. It wasn't based on spite or meanness or a desire to lash out at anyone. If you remember correctly, I didn't leave Love of my own accord. I was thrown out of this town like yesterday's garbage. Not a single person here wanted to hear what I had to say about the stolen money, nor did anyone consider how it must have felt to be standing in my shoes. I was the town pariah. So when I found out I was pregnant with Emma after leaving here, the very last thing I ever wanted to do was come back to this town."

"Or to me?" The reality of it wounded him. Things had been so bad between them she'd chosen to raise Emma alone rather than share the experience with him. That knowledge shattered him.

Paige's mouth hardened. "That wasn't an option. You made that quite clear when you turned your back on me. If I remember correctly, you told me to leave town, said there wasn't anything for me in Love."

"I turned my back on you?" Cameron asked, feeling incredulous at Paige's spin on things. "You knew where your father went when he left town with all our money and you refused to tell me or anybody else," he protested. "You protected him!"

Paige angrily brushed away tears. "I didn't know his whereabouts until much later. He was my father. No matter what you thought of him, he was my only living parent. And I didn't know for certain where he'd gone or what he'd done. He fled town without saying a word to me. I had my suspicions, but no facts. And this town wanted blood. When they couldn't produce my father, they went after me."

Cameron winced inwardly as memories from those terrible days washed over him. He'd been so outraged and jaded and shocked by Robert's duplicity that he'd been numb to Paige's pain. It had been an impossible situation. And he still didn't know how much or how little Paige had known about her father's scam. For some reason it had been easier to believe that she too had betrayed him, even though he had always known Paige to be an honorable woman.

"Tensions ran high. I'll admit that," Cameron said. "People were hurt and devastated and furious. But no matter what went down between the two of us, you owed me the truth about Emma. I had a right to know she was part of this world."

"That's one of the main reasons why I'm here, Cameron. Losing my father made me realize that I have no right to keep you from knowing your daughter. Because warts and all, I adored my father. I'm thankful he was in my life. And I want you to have the chance of having the same relationship with Emma."

He was trying not to lose his temper, but hearing

her talk about the man who'd nearly bankrupted Love grated on his nerves. He didn't want to hear about her great love for her father when he'd missed fourteen months of his daughter's life. Not when Robert had hurt the people Cameron cared about most in this world and taught him a brutal lesson about betrayal.

"I can appreciate that, but don't expect anyone else in town to echo those sentiments. Your father was a thief and a liar. He deceived this entire town. And now, because of him, I lost out on moments with Emma that I'll never get back. The moment she started crawling. Her first steps. Her first word."

She jutted her chin out. "You lost out on those moments because of my choices and your own actions. My father may have been dishonorable, but he didn't wreck our relationship. We did that all on our own."

Paige's words slithered inside him like a poisonous viper. Was Paige trying to make him responsible for her poor decision? Was she once again deflecting blame from her father? And onto him?

Suddenly all he felt was fatigue. The news about Emma being his daughter had left him reeling. He'd got way more than he'd ever imagined when he set off to track Paige down at the homestead. What he needed right now was some time alone with his thoughts. He needed God as a sounding board as he worked through this situation.

He pinched the bridge of his nose. "I think it's time I left, Paige. I came here tonight to get answers about the funds you mentioned wanting to return to the town. Let's leave this discussion for another time."

Paige nodded. "I agree. It's late, and we could probably go round and round this issue for hours. Nothing has really changed in two years between us." A sigh slipped past her lips. "Although I know I've changed. I like to think I'm a better person now, one who's grounded in her faith and her values. Two years ago God wasn't a factor in my life, but now He's my anchor."

Her faith? God? Two years ago Paige's beliefs had been nonexistent. Much like his own. During their relationship neither of them had been leading a faith-based life. Matter of fact, he couldn't remember a single time they had attended church or prayed together. Faith had not been a part of their lives.

He nodded. "I can appreciate that. I've turned my life over to God, as well."

Paige opened the front door for him. Her expression was shuttered. He stood on the threshold, his body half-turned toward her. He bowed his head down for a moment, then swung his gaze up to meet her scrutiny. "You're wrong about nothing changing, Paige. Emma changes everything. From this moment forward, my life is never going to be the same. I wish you had seen fit to tell me about her fourteen months ago."

He charged off into the night, not even waiting for Paige to respond. His heart and mind were filled with a hundred different emotions. Fear gripped him. What if he wasn't cut out for fatherhood? What if it was too late to bond with Emma? Despite those questions, the major emotion he felt was pride in the chubby-cheeked beauty who bore a stunning resemblance to him. However, her mama made him want to scream with frustration and yell at the top of his lungs. She made him feel other things, too. Tender sentiments that tempted him to reach out and caress her cheek or plant a sweet kiss on her lips. It had been entirely too long since romantic feelings had swept over him. It was safe to say he missed those moments.

Even after all this time, Paige made him feel things he had thought were dead and buried in his stone-cold heart. Things he had no intention of resurrecting.

Paige stood in the doorway and watched as Cameron roared off into the darkness. She wrapped her arms around her middle as the wind whipped straight through her. When she could no longer see his taillights, she headed back inside the house. Seeing Cameron so turned upside down left her feeling guilt-ridden and sad. What had she expected? She had dropped a bombshell on him with no warning. He had been blindsided.

It wasn't as if they were close. The love they had once shared had died out years ago. All they shared in the present was a precious child.

Although she knew she had done the right thing in returning to Love, it didn't feel like it at the moment. So much time had passed, yet Cameron was still consumed by anger and bitterness. Would he be able to put those emotions aside in order to co-parent with her? To be the father Emma deserved?

Stay the course. It was her mother's expression, one she'd used often during Paige's upbringing. Emma Reynolds had been a firm believer in sticking to a plan and seeing it to its fruition. *Don't give up so easily.* Her mother's voice washed over her like a welcoming summer breeze.

She smiled to herself, knowing that once again her mother was sharing her wisdom, even though she was no longer with her. It made her feel not so alone in the world. It gave her courage.

With the large sum of money she now had and a plan to resurrect the cannery deal, Paige knew she could help revitalize this town. If Cameron agreed to join forces with her, they would be unstoppable. But after being bamboozled by her father, she had no idea whether he would ever agree to take this journey with her. And finding out about Emma might just have convinced him that she couldn't be trusted.

Lord, please let Cameron see Emma as a blessing in his life. And please don't let his anger over the past blind him to the possibilities for the future.

As she headed to her bedroom to turn in for the night, she couldn't help but peek in on her baby girl. She soundlessly entered the room, praying the floorboards wouldn't creak as she tiptoed toward the bed. Emma was curled up on her side, sleeping soundly. Her little thumb was rooted in her mouth. Paige's chest tightened with raw emotion. What she felt could never be expressed with mere words. It was the purest form of love. Instinctual. Maternal. And more than anything in the world, she wanted to give Cameron the opportunity to bond with Emma so that he too could feel this way about his daughter. Emma deserved two loving parents.

Tomorrow she would seek him out again. This time, though, she was bringing Emma to town with her. There was no way she was going to hide her daughter away like a dirty little secret.

* * *

Cameron fidgeted with the coffee machine, his nerves teetering on the edge as he made the first batch of the day. On a normal morning the scent of coffee wafting in the air served as a shot of adrenaline to his senses. But after last night he was going to need a mega shot of espresso to get him going. He couldn't seem to focus on the day-to-day tasks that he usually performed like clockwork. It had started with him fumbling over the keys to the Moose Café. It had taken him several tries to find the right one to fit the lock. And judging by the taste of this coffee, he'd messed up his usual process. His mind was somewhere else.

Had he dreamed up the events of last night?

Was he really and truly the father of a little girl?

Emma Prescott. For the first time since he'd found out he was a father, it hit him that his nephew, Aidan, now had a cousin. Aidan, the son of his brother Liam, was about to turn four years old. In his mind's eye he could see the two of them becoming buddies and playmates. Maybe even going skating on Deer Run Lake or tobogganing out in Nottingham Woods as they grew older.

Whoa. He needed to slow down before he made any plans about the future. He had a hard time imagining Paige relocating to Love. He chewed his lip. How could he maintain a decent relationship with Emma if they lived back in Seattle? A twinge of doubt speared through him as he recalled how terribly Paige had been treated in the aftermath of the scandal. And he'd done absolutely nothing to intervene or make things better.

He'd been too busy licking his wounds and dealing with angry townsfolk.

What might have been if Robert hadn't conceived a twisted scheme to fleece the town? And if there hadn't been so much suspicion thrown in Paige's direction?

"Morning, Cameron. Isn't it gorgeous outside?" A chirpy voice rang out behind him. "All that fresh Alaskan air is so invigorating. It's like I used to say when I lived in Saskell—if I could bottle up fresh air, I could make a fortune."

He swung his gaze up from his rank cup of coffee. His employee Sophie Miller looked as bright and fresh as a daisy. That was Sophie through and through. A regular burst of sunshine peeking out from the clouds. With her red hair and green eyes, she was striking in a girl-next-door kind of way.

Cameron grunted a greeting. He hadn't got more than a few hours' sleep last night and he felt as foul-tempered as a grizzly bear. Sophie's upbeat personality might just kill him today.

"Well, good morning to you, too, Mr. Grumpypants. I do believe somebody got up on the wrong side of the bed." She wagged her finger at him as if he were a small child rather than her boss. Sophie had come to Love courtesy of the Operation Love campaign started by Jasper. With her Southern accent and sweet-as-pie personality, she was a favorite with all his customers and the residents. Best friends with his sister-in-law, Grace, she knew her way around a coffeehouse like nobody's business.

"Who's grumpy?" Hazel barked as she appeared in the kitchen doorway. "Not Prince Charming here?"

Sophie jutted her chin in his direction. She adjusted her apron around her waist and began prepping her work area.

"Cameron Prescott! You're too blessed to be cantankerous," Hazel said, planting a hand on her hip.

Cameron rolled his eyes at her. "Says the woman who's dating my grandfather, the most ornery man on the planet."

Hazel grinned from ear to ear. She was practically glowing. "He's downright sweet with me. Tender. Romantic. And he's a good kisser to boot."

He shuddered. "Hazel. Do me a favor and never mention anything even remotely related to the two of you kissing. Never ever again."

Hazel began humming a lively tune as she sauntered over to a table and greeted the day's first customers with lively banter. Cameron couldn't help but laugh. Sophie and Hazel sure did keep things interesting around the café. They were an important part of the success of his establishment. He still needed a replacement for Grace, who'd returned to journalism full-time after a brief stint as a barista.

As customers trickled in, Cameron busied himself taking orders and making specialty coffee drinks. Time passed quickly as the morning crowd dissipated and he began the prep work for the lunch rush. A quick glance at his watch sent a feeling of dread coursing through him. It was almost noontime! Lately it seemed as if Jasper and Boone showed up like clockwork for the lunch specials. The sheriff's office was located right across the street, so Boone didn't have far to travel. Knowing his grandfather, he was champing at the bit to find out the particulars about his conversation with Paige last night. As it was, he had a whole lot more to tell his family than they could ever imagine. He felt a smile tugging at the corners of his lips as Emma's sweet face popped into his mind.

At twelve thirty, his hunch about his family showing up at his establishment proved to be accurate as Jasper, Boone and Grace came in and settled down at one of the bigger tables toward the back of the café.

"Hazel, are Boone and Jasper here to talk about Paige and the money?" Cameron asked with an exasperated sigh. He didn't need this right now. He was trying to run a successful business. A table full of Prescotts never boded well. Now was not the time to discuss Paige's return to Love or the idea she'd presented to him about the cannery. Besides, he had more pressing matters at hand. He had to find a way to tell them about Emma. And he wasn't about to do it in front of all his regular customers so it would become the talk of the town.

Sophie was over at the table, taking their orders and laughing at something Jasper was saying to her. She threw back her head and chuckled, pulled in by Jasper's charm.

"What do I look like? A mind reader?" Hazel grunted. "Go on over and ask them yourself."

Knowing he had to deal with them sooner rather than later, Cameron headed over to his family.

"Hey, guys. Fancy seeing you all here," Cameron drawled.

"Hey, Cam. I'm loving the new additions to the menu," Grace said with a smile. "It's making me nostalgic."

"Thanks, Gracie," Cameron said, not missing the way his brother reached out and touched his wife's stomach. He had the feeling a baby announcement would be coming any day now. For now, he would just pretend he hadn't noticed the warm gesture. He winked at his sister-in-law. "Your barista position is still open if you're interested," he teased.

"Sophie is ten times the barista I ever was," Grace admitted, giving Sophie a thumbs-up sign, making the young woman blush prettily. "Besides, I'm too busy writing about the great state of Alaska. Matter of fact, I can't stay. I'm on deadline, so I'm grabbing a coffee to go." She stood up to leave, then leaned down and brushed a tender kiss across Boone's lips. With a parting smile, she walked over to the counter and picked up her coffee, then headed outdoors into the afternoon sunshine.

Cameron shoved his hands in his front pockets and looked nervously around the table. Jasper and Boone were staring at him as if they were waiting for breaking news. "Listen, guys. I need to talk to you all about something. This place is packed right now, so I'd like to do it at a more private moment. Maybe we can grab some dinner at my house and invite Liam and Honor to come, as well."

"Is it about the money?" Jasper asked, leaning forward across the table. His eyes were glistening with excitement.

"No," he said with a frown directed at his grandfather. "It's not about the money. This is…personal."

"Whatever works for you, Cam. We're here to support you, no matter what," Boone asserted.

Jasper nodded. "That's pretty much the reason we came by here today. We know it's not easy to have Paige back in town."

"Thanks, guys," he said, fighting to speak past the huge lump in his throat. He didn't know what in the world was wrong with him. It was a rare occasion when he let his emotions get the best of him. A long time ago he'd learned to stuff them down so no one could see his hurts. He considered it his special power.

The loud jangling of the bell hanging over the Moose Café's entrance announced the arrival of customers. Turning his head to greet them, Cameron froze as he instantly recognized the honey-blond hair and the heart-shaped face that never failed to make his pulse quicken. Paige had just sailed through the door of the Moose Café with his look-alike daughter cradled against her chest.

Knowing his worlds were about to collide, Cameron dived right in. "I have something to tell you," he said, looking back and forth between Boone and Jasper. "Paige didn't come back solo. She brought my daughter with her."

Jasper's eyes bulged and he began coughing. Boone's jaw slacked.

His grandfather sputtered. "What are you talking about?"

Cameron met Jasper's harsh gaze without flinching. "That little girl over there is mine."

"Ha! Is that what she told you?" Jasper grunted. "It's been almost two years since you saw that woman. I wouldn't trust a word that comes out of her mouth."

Cameron clenched his teeth. "That woman has a name. It's Paige. I expect you to settle down and treat her with the respect she deserves."

"R-respect?" Jasper sputtered. "After what she and her father pulled?"

"Regardless of what she may have done, she's still the mother of my child." He ground out the words with a fierceness that surprised him.

Jasper waved his hand at Cameron. "You always had a soft spot for that—"

"Don't finish that sentence!" He glared at Jasper. "And if you can't manage to pull it together, it's probably best that you leave my establishment."

As Cameron turned away from Jasper and began to walk toward Paige and Emma, he felt a surge of triumph rise up inside him. Jasper's comments highlighted the fact that Paige was still under a cloud of suspicion. Most here in Love wouldn't welcome her back. Cameron himself still had major questions and doubts about her involvement in the embezzlement scheme. Standing up to Jasper wasn't about any lingering feelings he had for Paige. He'd fallen out of love with her a long time ago. It was now all about his innocent daughter, who didn't deserve to be pulled under by a town scandal and enmity for her mother.

Regardless of what Jasper thought, it wasn't about

defending the woman he had once loved. It was about safeguarding the baby whom he now felt duty-bound to protect.

Chapter Four

As soon as Paige had stepped into the Moose Café, she'd felt an electric current simmering in the air. Although she hadn't been nervous a few minutes ago, there was a sudden fluttering sensation low in her belly. Maybe this hadn't been a good idea after all. Familiar faces jumped out at her. Folks she'd known for years became wide-eyed at the sight of her. A few of them even whispered behind their hands and pointed at Emma, causing her to snuggle her daughter even closer against her chest. From across the room her eyes locked with Cameron. He wasn't alone. Even though she'd known it might happen sooner than she'd like, the sight of his brother and grandfather hit her like a ton of bricks.

The past and the present blurred as memories from two years ago assailed her senses. As town mayor, Jasper had led the outrage against the daughter of Robert Reynolds. It hadn't mattered to him that they'd known each for years or that she was his grandson's longtime girlfriend. As town sheriff, Boone had grilled her with questions about the embezzlement of the funds. Throughout the grueling process she'd told them the truth—she'd known nothing about her father's criminal acts. She was innocent, even though no one had believed in her.

She inhaled a deep breath, reminding herself that she'd chosen to walk this path of redemption and reconciliation. No matter how unpleasant, she was going to keep trying to make a difference in Love, and, in the process, serve as a positive role model for Emma.

Before she knew it, Cameron was at her side, his gaze focused on Emma. His eyes flickered with an emotion that resembled pride. Her daughter reached out a chubby hand and tugged at Cameron's chin. The gesture surprised Paige since Emma always seemed so finicky with strangers. In response, Cameron let out a throaty chuckle, which made Emma giggle. She winced at the notion that her daughter didn't know her own father, even though she appeared to be taking to him like a duck to water. *From this point forward,* she vowed, *these two will be in each other's lives. Girls always need their daddies.*

"Do they know about Emma?" Paige asked, her eyes darting nervously toward the back of the café. Hazel was now standing at the table, a stunned expression etched on her face. She swung her eyes toward Paige.

"I just briefly filled them in. I'd like them to meet her. Are you all right with going over there?" Cameron asked, his gaze intense as he studied her face.

"Of course," she said, knowing this meeting had been inevitable in a town this size. And the sooner she crossed these bridges, the sooner she could start working toward resurrecting the cannery deal and returning a portion of the stolen money. Her goals wouldn't be achieved by avoiding awkward encounters. Feeling as if all eyes were on her, Paige followed behind Cameron as he led her to the back table.

With her head held high, she met Jasper's mistrustful gaze steadily. She felt her chin wobbling under the pressure but she held her ground.

"Well, Miss Paige Reynolds, I must say I never thought our paths would cross again," Jasper drawled. His silver eyebrows danced above his eyes. He opened his mouth, then quickly shut it. Something told her she wouldn't have enjoyed whatever he'd stopped himself from blurting out. The mayor of Love was well-known for his caustic wit.

"Hello, Paige," Boone greeted her. "It's been a long time." His expression didn't give much away, although his eyes radiated wariness.

"Boone," she said with a nod. "Two years, to be exact."

Boone took a step toward her and reached for Emma's chubby finger. "Well, who do we have here?" he asked in a soft voice.

"Her name is Emma," Paige said. "Emma Prescott."

She felt the heat of Cameron's gaze as he studied her. Was that a pleased expression on his face? She wasn't quite certain, but it sure looked like it. So far, Cameron seemed to be handling the situation pretty well. Even though he'd been surprised by the news last night, his reaction had been one of acceptance, despite his anger at her for waiting so long to reveal the truth. This was the true Cameron. Upstanding. Mature. Honorable.

Thank You, Lord, for allowing Cameron to see Emma

as a gift and not a hindrance. She's the light of my world, so I'm praying she'll be a ray of sunshine in his.

"She looks just like you, Cam," Boone said, a smile playing around his lips. "Much better-looking, of course."

Cameron's grin widened. Emma couldn't take her eyes off him. It was as if her daddy were the sun, the moon and the stars. Paige sighed. Once upon a time she had thought the same thing about Cameron. And he'd proved her faith in him time after time, until in one terrible moment he had betrayed their love. She winced at the recollection of how coldly Cameron had treated her. Being innocent hadn't spared her from the town's or Cameron's judgment and scorn.

After all this time it still wounded her to remember those dark days. The scars were still there, whether or not anyone cared to acknowledge them.

"I won't even argue that point with you, Boone. Emma is by far the best-looking Prescott," Cameron said, earning himself a pat on the back from Boone.

Paige felt as if a weight had been lifted off her shoulders as she watched the easy camaraderie between Cameron and his brother. She'd once been friends with Boone, so it was a relief that he didn't seem to be shunning her. Or Emma. It would mean so much for her daughter's future to have tight family connections in Love. Jasper, on the other hand, appeared as frosty as Mount McKinley in the dead of winter. Gritting her teeth, she reminded herself to make the best of the awkward situation.

"How old is the little one?" Jasper asked, jutting his chin in Emma's direction.

"Fourteen months," she answered, biting back the impulse to tell Jasper his great-granddaughter had a name.

"You shouldn't hold her so much," Jasper said with a furrowed brow, moving quickly toward Paige and reaching for Emma. "Set her down on the ground. Let her get her bearings." Before Paige could protest, Jasper had plucked Emma from her arms and settled her on the floor.

Paige bristled. Who did Jasper think he was to interfere with her mothering?

Emma let out a high-pitched giggle and began to occupy herself with the wooden leg of a chair, seemingly fascinated by the texture of it. As usual, she was delighted with the world around her and all it had to offer.

"I don't want her to fall," Paige fretted. So far in Emma's young life she and Fiona had been the only ones she could depend on for all her needs. It had always been mother and daughter against the world. It only stood to reason that she was a little overprotective with regards to her daughter.

"She'll be fine tottering around here. I'll keep an eye on her," Hazel said in a voice as sweet as honey. She was looking down at Emma with a rapturous smile. It was amazing, Paige thought, how a tiny tot could warm up even the most obstinate of hearts.

Cameron nodded at her, letting her know without words that Emma was fine under Hazel's supervision. With her heart in her throat, Paige watched as Emma walked off with Hazel following closely behind her.

Even though she was only a few feet away, Paige found herself checking to make sure her daughter was all right.

"Why don't we all sit down," Cameron suggested. He pulled out a chair and gestured with his hand for her to take a seat. She blinked in surprise. Cameron had always been a gentleman, a trait that had endeared him to her. He had dedicated himself to the courtly gestures. Flowers. Sweet notes. Balloons on her birthday. She let out a sigh as she sat down. It had been a long time since anyone had held a chair out for her or surprised her with an armful of forget-me-nots, the official Alaska state flower.

Boone, Jasper and Cameron all settled into their seats. She hadn't bothered the night before, but Paige now took a moment to look around at the decor of the café. It was an assortment of neutral colors—browns, grays and burnished copper. Antlers hung on the wall alongside retro Alaskan art. A sweet picture of the Prescotts as kids—Cameron, Honor, Boone and Liam—held a place of honor by the counter. A bubbly titian-haired waitress wove in and out of the tables, pouring coffee and taking orders. The place pulsed with a vibrant energy.

Her stomach rumbled in appreciation of the enticing aromas emanating through the café. Cameron had always been an excellent cook. On many a date night he'd invited her over to his house for a delicious home-cooked meal. A smile played on her lips as she remembered his most ambitious dish. Beef Bourguignonne. A meal they had enjoyed by candlelight and good conversation. Laughter had flowed through the air like oxygen. Sometimes it seemed as if those days had belonged to another couple, not two people who no longer seemed to know one another.

"So, it seems you had several reasons to come back to Love in addition to introducing Cameron to Emma. He told us that you intend to return some of the money to the town," Boone said. "I have to say I'm surprised. The money was stolen two years ago."

Paige held Boone's gaze. Anger radiated from his eyes.

"It's the right thing to do. I've already written the check out to the town. Unfortunately, a portion of it was spent by my father. However, there's a good deal of it left." Paige dug in her purse and pulled out the check she'd endorsed to the town of Love. She slid it across the table toward Jasper.

Jasper's eyes bulged as he picked it up and looked it over. A strangled sound slipped past his lips. Boone and Cameron leaned in to get a glimpse of the check.

Cameron swung his gaze to her. His expression was one of awe. "This is a game changer for the town. Thank you, Paige."

His tender tone filled her with warmth. His face had lost all of its hard edges. For a moment it sent her back to a time when he'd been her entire world. It felt reassuring to know that despite everything, the man she had once loved was still lurking there under his harsh facade. He hadn't completely disappeared.

Jasper let out a hoot and clapped his hands together. "Even the darkest of deeds can't triumph over this town."

She nodded her head in agreement. "I'm hoping it

can really help with Love's economy. It's something I've prayed about for months now. Being able to salvage the cannery deal could be a financial boon."

Jasper's expression became cloudy. "The cannery deal! What are you talking about? We had to put that to rest two years ago after your father robbed us blind." Jasper's voice rang out sharply. Paige felt her cheeks heat with embarrassment. She felt certain other nearby diners had heard Jasper's comment. Several swiveled their heads in the direction of their table.

"Jasper!" Cameron said in a warning tone. "Knock it off!"

Jasper frowned at Cameron. "I'm merely stating the obvious. Robert Reynolds did this town a world of harm. He was like a Category 3 hurricane that raged through Love, leaving nothing but destruction in his wake. I'm not going to walk on eggshells about that fact."

Paige took a few calming breaths. Jasper had every right to be upset about her father's misdeeds. She just hadn't expected him to be so crotchety about everything. It was a good thing she was used to dealing with cantankerous men like Jasper Prescott. During her father's illness he'd been short-tempered and impatient at times. Through it all she'd cared for him as any loving daughter would do, using every ounce of compassion and patience she had in her being. Even if it killed her, she would show Jasper the same grace she'd bestowed on her father. After all, he was Emma's great-grandfather.

A verse from Hebrews ran through her mind, reassuring her about the way she wished to respond to Jasper. *Let us then with confidence draw near to the throne of grace, that we may receive mercy and find grace to help in time of need.*

She had returned to Love in order to help all the townsfolk, even a cranky senior citizen who didn't seem to care one little bit about her own feelings. He was about as subtle as a sledgehammer. In his eyes she was still complicit in her father's crimes. Paige knew she needed thick skin to deal with him. It was about the town's prosperity, she reminded herself, not about her hurt feelings.

"I understand why you feel that way, Jasper," she said in a soothing voice. "Things went horribly awry the first time around. But that doesn't mean the town can't revisit the cannery deal now that there's going to be an infusion of cash."

"Paige is right," Cameron said. "The project exhilarated this town. And it would have been a shot of adrenaline for the economy. We're still struggling to get out of this financial downturn, Jasper. A cannery right here in Love might open up a world of possibilities."

Jasper shook his head. "I've never been one to look backward. If we want to revitalize the economy, we have to move forward."

"It's still a viable plan," Paige insisted. "Please don't discount it because you disapprove of the messenger."

Jasper began to sputter. "This isn't personal, although I would be remiss in not saying that having you on board any town project would be quite controversial."

Paige had prepared herself for this type of rejection, but it still stung to be treated like an outsider when Love had been her home for so many years. Over the course of the past two years she had missed it like crazy. The villagers. Her friends. The sights, sounds and smells. And the Prescotts, who had made her an honorary member of their family. And most of all, she had missed Cameron and the loving relationship they'd shared.

Just at that moment Emma walked back to their table, with Hazel right on her heels. She had a sweet smile on her face as she toddled up to Paige with her arms outstretched.

Paige reached down and lifted Emma up into her lap. Emma grinned at her, revealing her two front teeth. They'd come in a few months ago, giving both mother and daughter many a sleepless night due to teething pain. Cameron reached over and tickled Emma under her chin. In response, she let loose with a high-pitched squeal. The look on Jasper's face didn't escape Paige's notice. He couldn't keep his eyes off Emma. Jasper Prescott was a man who valued family ties and legacy and connections. It would be only a matter of time before her daughter won him over.

"If it's all right with you, Paige, I was going to get Emma a glass of apple juice and some cheese crackers for a snack." Hazel's eyes oozed affection. Her tone was conciliatory.

"Sure," Paige said with a smile. "She would love that. Let me get her sippy cup." Paige reached down, and after rooting around in her diaper bag for the cup, she handed it to Hazel.

"Coming right up," Hazel chirped as she walked off toward the kitchen. It seemed that Hazel's heart had been softened by Emma, Paige realized. Relief flooded her. It was so much nicer to have Hazel treating her with warmth rather than censure.

"We're having a town meeting on Wednesday night," Boone said, returning to the issue at hand. "Perhaps this is something we should address with the council. It's worth exploring, especially now that Operation Love is shining a spotlight on our village."

Jasper sat back in his chair and folded his arms across his chest. He locked gazes with her. "I don't want to hurt your feelings, especially now that you've brought my sweet great-granddaughter back to her roots, but I'm not sure this town would ever want you at the helm of any business deal."

"Why not?" Paige asked in a slightly defiant tone. "I have a business degree and I know everything there is to know about the cannery deal."

Jasper let out a hoot. "Why not? What a question. The sins of the father are often visited on the child. Small towns have a habit of holding grudges."

Cameron folded his arms on the table. He scowled at Jasper. "Small towns? Or small-town mayors?"

Jasper slammed his palm down on the table. "Don't act all high and mighty with me! You weren't exactly protesting Paige's innocence two years ago, now were you?"

A shocked silence descended on the table. Cameron glowered at Jasper. Boone looked at their grandfather and shook his head disapprovingly. Paige held tightly on to Emma and prayed her daughter wouldn't pick up on the tension at the table.

"You're right, Jasper," Cameron conceded. "I thought Paige was somehow involved in what happened."

Paige winced at Cameron's blunt statement. It burned her insides every time the knowledge washed over her that he didn't believe in her. It was yet another reason that she had doubts about living in Love. There was no way she wanted Emma to grow up knowing her own father doubted the integrity of her mother.

"I would hope that Emma doesn't have to bear the brunt of any sins committed by Cameron or myself or her grandfather," Paige said in a cool, calm tone. "Judge not, lest ye be judged."

The air hung thick with discord. Out of nowhere Emma reached out and tugged hard at Jasper's beard. She let out a wild cackle.

Jasper's face held a stunned expression. His ice-blue eyes widened. Seconds later his shoulders began to shake, followed by his belly. He threw his head back as chortles of laughter rumbled through him. He swiped at his eyes with the back of his hand. "Bless her little heart. I think she's defending her mama. Okay, Little Miss Emma Prescott. I get your message loud and clear."

Cameron looked over at Paige and grinned at her. He reached out and smoothed his palm across Emma's cheek. His smile had a powerful impact on her. It nestled right inside her and yanked at the feelings she had buried a long time ago. Her heart began to flutter and she found herself feeling flushed, even though the temperature was quite comfortable inside the café.

"Let's introduce this at the town meeting. It's open

to the public, so there would be immediate feedback," Cameron suggested. He pointed in the direction of the check sitting on the table. "Jasper, you can present the check and open up the topic of how to best use the funds." He narrowed his gaze. "You could also make it clear that Paige returned to Love in order to return the money Robert stole."

Hazel appeared at the table and placed Emma's sippy cup in front of her. "That would endear her to a lot of folks," Hazel said. "And drive home the point that she's willing to move forward to help this town." She looked down at Paige, raw emotion shimmering in her eyes.

Jasper snorted. "The last time I checked, I'm still the mayor of this town. I'll decide how to address this at the town meeting." He jumped to his feet. "I need to get back to my office. Hazel, can you whip me up one of those turkey-and-avocado sandwiches to go?"

Without even saying a proper goodbye, Jasper reached for the check and stuffed it into his shirt pocket. He walked over to the counter with Hazel, his thoughts having presumably shifted to his lunch and away from the town's fiscal concerns. Paige shook her head at his abrupt departure. Just as it seemed she was making a little headway, Jasper had taken his marbles and left.

Boone checked his watch and let out a groan. "Looks like I need to head back to work, as well. Seems like I'm taking my lunch to go also." He nodded at Cameron, then Paige. He reached out his hand and stroked the top of Emma's head. "I'll be seeing you soon, cutie-pie. Can't wait for Gracie to meet you."

"He's a happily married man now," Cameron explained as Boone walked away. "In case you missed that telltale twinkle in his eye and the gushing tone in his voice."

"I happened to see their wedding announcement online. Their love story made quite a stir," she admitted, feeling a little sheepish about the fact that she'd been keeping tabs on the town. At the time she had felt happiness for Boone and sadness that she and Cameron hadn't gone the distance. "They seem like a great couple."

"They are," Cameron said with a nod. "I've never seen Boone happier."

"And how are Liam and Ruby? And Honor?" she asked. Although she felt as if she might be overstepping by posing the question, she was filled with curiosity about the remaining Prescott siblings. They had all been close once, and even though she had tried on numerous occasions, she couldn't just shut off her feelings. She still cared deeply about them.

Cameron's face blanched. All the light went out of his eyes. He began to stammer. "I—I can't pretty this up, Paige. Ruby passed away a year and a half ago."

Paige let out a gasp. Shock roared straight through her. Beautiful, strong Ruby. Everyone's friend. Wise sage. Warrior. Nurturer. "No! What happened? Was she ill?"

Cameron released a ragged breath. "She was killed in an avalanche search and rescue in Colorado. You know how Ruby was about saving lives. If there was an opportunity to help, she was there."

"I can't believe it." She choked out the words. Tears slid down her cheeks. She swiped them away with the back of her hand. Although she had kept tabs on the town, there had been a period of time after Emma's birth that she had been too occupied with her newborn baby to keep up with the major goings-on in Love. "I'm so sorry, Cam. For all of you, but especially for Liam and Aidan. I had no idea!" Impulsively, she reached out and clasped Cameron's hand. Seconds after making contact, she realized that touching Cameron hadn't been a good idea. Goose bumps had popped up on her forearms. For a moment tension hummed and buzzed in the air around them as they locked gazes.

"She died the way she lived. Heroically. Not that it eases the pain for Liam, but Ruby was a rock star as a search-and-rescue team member. My dad worked that rescue operation right alongside her. He said she saved several lives that day."

Paige remembered how Ruby had emailed her after she'd left Love. She'd been the one person who had attempted to reach out to her in kindness and friendship. They'd kept up communication until the emails had abruptly stopped on Ruby's end. It was devastating to realize that her friend's tragic death had been the reason for the lack of response to her messages. Paige had believed that Ruby's silence had indicated she no longer believed in her innocence.

"Losing someone without any kind of warning is so devastating," Paige said. Her father's terminal illness had been a terrible blow, but at least she'd had weeks and months to say goodbye to him. It had allowed her to process the loss as her father became sicker and sicker. She hadn't been completely blindsided. Ruby's tragic accident had been like a tsunami sweeping over the Prescott family. No warning. No chance to say goodbye. Just unimaginable loss.

"Liam is still struggling to get his life back. Aidan is still as sweet as ever. And Honor just graduated with her master's in wildlife conservation. She's back home now."

Paige shook her head, overwhelmed by how the wheels of life had kept moving in her absence. "It's amazing how much things can change in two years," she said.

Cameron darted a look at Emma, who was stuffing a portion of a cheese cracker in her mouth. "Tell me about it. This little one here drives that point home."

"Thank you," Paige said, trying to ignore the painful lump in her throat. Between the news about Ruby and Cameron's behavior earlier, she found herself becoming emotional.

Cameron drew his brows together. "For what?"

"For stepping in to plead my case with Jasper." She jiggled Emma on her lap. She hadn't expected him to be so solidly in her corner during the conversation with Jasper and Boone about the cannery. "For having my back even though I know you still have questions about my involvement with my father's crimes. And I know you must still be reeling from the news about Emma."

He shrugged. "Honestly, I wasn't pleading on your behalf. I was making a case for what's in the best interest of the town." He held her gaze. "You're the mother of my child, Paige. That in itself means we share an amazing connection, one that will last our whole lives. Lord knows we've had our differences, but going forward we have to present a united front for Emma. That's what parents do." His eyes hardened. "Does that mean all is forgiven or forgotten? No, of course not. I still question whether I can ever trust you."

She sucked in a deep breath. Despite already knowing he didn't trust her, his words hurt.

"You're right about focusing on Emma. That's what matters most." She looked down at her daughter and touched her curls. "I'd like to have Emma call you Daddy, if that's okay with you."

Cameron's eyes widened. His mouth swung open. "Of course it's all right. I—I'd be mighty proud to have her call me that," he said, his voice sounding husky. He reached for Emma's hand and brought it to his lips. "I'll see you later, princess. I need to get back to work before Hazel and Sophie get in the weeds with all these customers."

Paige tried to hide the disappointment that slithered through her. It had been so nice to spend time with Cameron, even if the majority of the time they had been discussing the cannery and the check she'd handed over to Jasper. She had missed having him in her life, plain and simple. It was obvious that Cameron was still holding her at arm's length even though he hadn't allowed his grandfather to run roughshod over her.

Baby steps, she reminded herself. One day soon Cameron would realize that he'd misjudged her.

"I should get going also. It's almost nap time," she said smoothly. She stood up and placed Emma on her hip while she reached for her purse.

"Let me help you," Cameron said, reaching for the diaper bag. He pretended to stagger under the weight of it. "You sure travel with a lot of stuff." He pulled out a stuffed elephant that was poking out of the bag. "Who's this guy?" he asked with a grin.

"Mine," Emma said, reaching for the stuffed animal. She pressed it against her chest. Her lip stuck out as she looked at Cameron with mistrust.

Paige and Cameron both began to chuckle at the ferocity with which Emma took ownership of her toy and her fierce expression. "She's very possessive of Mr. Snuggles and her stuffed bear, Lola. She doesn't even like to part with them when it's time for them to hit the washing machine," she teased, earning herself a grin in return.

"I'd like to spend some quality time with Emma. That way she can get used to me being around." He rubbed his chin. "I know it'll take some time, but I want her to know me. It's important that she recognizes me as her father."

"Of course," she said with a nod.

"I could take her to the upcoming spring festival. There's always something fun to do there."

"That should be fine," she said. "I'll be in touch." She took the diaper bag from Cameron's hand and slung it over her shoulder. After making sure Emma was fully bundled up in her coat and hat, she headed to the door. Once again, curious stares seemed to greet her as she walked out of the Moose Café. *Let them stare!* All they cared about was town gossip and rumors. They had no idea that she was back in town with a purpose. Her love for her father dictated that she uphold his dying wish of redemption. And her newfound faith had shown her that separating a man from his child was wrong.

A sliver of fear crept down her spine. Although it had been one of her goals to introduce Cameron to his daughter in the hopes that they would forge a relationship, the idea of Emma and Cameron bonding made her feel vulnerable. She had always been the custodial parent, the one who did all the nurturing and heavy lifting. Emma was all she had in the world. What might happen if Cameron got married and decided he wanted to raise Emma? What would she do if Emma decided down the road that she wanted to be a part of the big, bustling Prescott family? All she had to offer her daughter was herself. There was no one else. No uncles or aunts. Or grandparents. No bells or whistles. In many ways, Cameron could offer Emma a much fuller life than she ever could.

Paige knew her feelings were selfish, but she couldn't control the growing tide of anxiety. As a single mother, she had always felt vulnerable. Giving her daughter a full, richly textured life was essential to Emma's wellbeing. It was something she'd prayed over on many occasions. That God would allow Emma to be loved abundantly. Now all her fears were rising to the surface and bubbling over. The truth was hard to ignore. It caused her stomach to get all tied up in knots. If she lost her precious Emma, she wouldn't have a single thing left in her world. She would be completely and utterly alone.

Chapter Five

⌒

A small town like Love didn't harbor many secrets. By the time Cameron opened up the Moose Café the next morning, the entire village had heard about Paige's return and the fact that she had brought back a baby who was his spitting image. His phone had been ringing off the hook since last night with inquiries from concerned citizens and well-meaning friends. Add in a few town gossips and his head had been spinning with all the attention being directed his way.

Paige's name was on the tip of everyone's tongue. Even gentle-hearted Honor had been up in arms, especially when he had confirmed the fact that he was Emma's father.

Last night Paige had reached out to him about meeting up over at the site of the unfinished cannery building. She had mentioned something about getting all her ducks lined up in a row before the town council meeting. He'd reluctantly agreed to meet her this morning after he opened up the café and made sure Sophie and

Hazel could hold down the fort. Still, after all this time, he found it almost impossible to say no to her. Although he respected Paige for wanting to make things right, he wasn't sure of his role in her grand plan. A long time ago he had made peace about the fact that instead of being involved with the running of a cannery, he was now owner of a popular and profitable eatery. God had shown him that when one door slammed shut on him, another one had opened up with wide-open arms.

The Moose Café had been his blessing after so many turbulent moments.

After parking in the makeshift lot next to the building, he got out of his truck and took a moment to survey his surroundings. The morning sun beating down on him felt incredible, as did the springlike temperatures Love was experiencing. The smell of the bay drifted toward him from the pier across the way, assailing his senses with a briny, salty aroma. He watched for a moment as a group of local fishermen made preparations to head off in search of a great day's haul. He felt a deep respect and admiration for fishermen. It was a rigorous, often dangerous job that was dependent on the elements. At times, circumstances were completely out of their control.

Cameron turned away from the pier and scanned the area for Paige. Within seconds he spotted her up on the hill facing the building that had been earmarked for the cannery. Emma was sitting on her hip wearing a pink coat and dark leggings. Just the sight of his daughter instantly brightened his day. He prayed that one day soon she would have an awareness of him as someone important in her life. There was nothing more powerful than a father in a young girl's world.

He felt a tightness in his chest as he surveyed the half-finished construction. Even now, the sight of it still hit him like a ton of bricks. It had held so much potential for greatness. All of it had gone up in a puff of smoke. "And for what?" he grumbled to himself. Greed and misplaced values.

"Morning, Paige," Cameron said as he walked up the incline to where she was standing. "Good morning, beautiful," he crooned as he tweaked Emma's nose. The little girl buried her face against her mother's chest, then peeked her head out to look at him.

Paige watched the interaction between the two of them, her face lit up like sunshine. With not a hint of makeup on and her blond hair pulled into a high ponytail, she looked fresh-faced and radiant. She was dressed casually in a pair of dark jeans and a windbreaker. The April weather was unpredictable, ranging from light snow to balmy temperatures and lots of sunlight. At the moment it was glorious, if a bit breezy. After a frigid winter, the residents of Love deserved blue skies and warm sun.

"Thanks for meeting me. I've always liked the view from up here. You can look out and see Kachemak Bay and all the fishing boats." Her mouth quirked. "A part of me was hoping I'd walk up to the site and see that the construction had been finished." Emma tugged at Paige's hand with her chubby fingers.

"That wasn't possible. The town didn't have the money to complete the project," he said in a sharper voice than he'd intended. The subject was a tricky one, considering they both knew why the funds hadn't been available. Robert Reynolds's deception had caused so many ripples throughout Love. Paige hadn't remained in town long enough to see all the damage firsthand.

Paige pointed in the direction of the building. "I'm wondering if the original plan for this building can be scaled down if the town decides to move forward with the project. I think it could be a lot more cost-effective and the cannery could get up and running sooner if the construction is scaled back."

Had Paige been staying up at night thinking all this through? It was impressive but a bit premature in his opinion. The project was a long way from being greenlighted. He wasn't so sure Paige realized that it was far from being a done deal.

"That's a good point," he said. "The original blueprints were a bit ambitious."

"This building represented so much. Hopes. Dreams." Paige let out a sigh. "The future of this town was all wrapped up in this factory."

"You and I had plans for the future. And lots of dreams," Cameron blurted out. He didn't know why he'd thrown that out there, but he was tired of pretending as if his life hadn't been derailed by events that had been out of his control. He was tired of guarding his heart due to Paige.

"Yes, we did," she acknowledged. There was a wistful edge to her voice. "We had lots of plans. It seems like a lifetime ago."

She was right. It had been a long time since he had allowed himself to remember all they had shared. They'd talked about settling down and building a house with a clear view of the mountains. That particular dream of hearth and home had been difficult to say goodbye to. Because of her business background and his own entrepreneurial sensibilities, they had tossed around ideas of creating their own enterprise. At the time it had seemed as if their lives had been ripe with such promise. Such incredible hope now turned to ash.

A bitter taste rose in his mouth as reality washed over him. None of it had come to pass. That knowledge caused an ache that threatened to pull him under. Suddenly he was eager to get away from Paige before he succumbed to the push and pull of their beautiful memories. Loving Paige had once caused him a world of hurt and pain. Falling back in love with her wasn't an option. It had taken him years to finally get over the loss of her. He couldn't afford to believe again in the possibility of the two of them. He had no interest in having the rug pulled out from under him again.

"Why did you want to meet me out here?" he asked in a clipped tone. He didn't intend to linger here with her at the site of his colossal failure.

Paige juggled a fidgety Emma in her arms. "Because so far, you're my only ally here in Love and I wanted to toss some ideas around with you." Emma held up her hands to Cameron and he happily transferred her to his arms. Just having her snuggled against his chest made it hard for him to focus on the subject at hand.

Ally? How could he ever be one to someone he didn't trust? Paige's withholding the information about Emma had cemented the cold, hard fact that she couldn't be counted on.

He shook his head. "I wouldn't exactly say that. Just because I stepped in with Jasper doesn't mean we're a united front. This is separate and apart from Emma. While I definitely see the positive aspects of resurrecting the cannery deal, there are also several drawbacks."

Her face fell. "But I thought you, of all people, would support this plan. You lived, breathed and dreamed about building a cannery for years."

He blew out a frustrated sigh. Paige didn't need to remind him of that fact. "Yes, I did. But sometimes we have to come to terms with the reality that not all of our dreams come to fruition."

Paige frowned at him. "Is this about my integrity? Is that why you have reservations?"

All of a sudden he was wishing he'd passed on her invitation to join her this morning, although holding Emma in his arms was worth it. This wasn't a road he wanted to go down. He'd made up his mind to keep things civil with Paige for Emma's sake. But he knew it wasn't wise to put his faith in her. The ache of her betrayal served as a constant reminder.

"That's a loaded question. And a little bit unfair since I'm still processing being a father to a child I knew nothing about until a few days ago." He gazed into Emma's innocent eyes. She was studying him with a look of curiosity etched on her face. "Dada," he said, placing her tiny little hand against his chest. "Dada."

Paige sucked in a deep breath. "I was wrong keeping Emma from you, Cameron. I'm willing to say that with one hundred percent accountability. So far you've admitted no culpability in anything." Paige's features tightened. A small furrow appeared on her brow. "Is it so hard to say you might have been wrong about me?"

Cameron chewed the inside of his cheek. The truth was there had been more reasons to disbelieve Paige about her involvement in the embezzlement scheme than reasons to believe in her innocence. After so long it would be difficult to do a complete turnaround. Facing the fact that he had been wrong would mean taking responsibility for the events that had led to her leaving town and giving birth to his daughter in secret.

He clenched his jaw. "My reservations about the cannery are based on practical matters that have nothing to do with your character or our past relationship."

"Well, that's at least something," Paige cracked.

Cameron glanced at his watch. "I hate to run without being able to help you very much, but we've got a crisis brewing at the café. Both Sophie and one of my new hires are out sick today with a stomach bug. Hazel is holding down the fort for me, but I'm guessing it's going to be a madhouse soon, what with the lunch crowd coming in."

"I can fill in for them, Cameron. In case you've forgotten, I waitressed all through college."

Cameron studied Paige's earnest expression. He knew she was determined to undo the wrongs of the past, but did she really want to subject herself to customers who might still be harboring animosity toward her and her father? It was way above and beyond the call of duty. It seemed like a surefire way to get her feelings hurt.

"I don't doubt your waitressing skills," he admitted, a smile threatening to break out on his face at the thought of Paige wearing one of the café's moose T-shirts. "It might get rough with some of the townsfolk."

Paige straightened her shoulders and lifted her chin up. "I'm tougher than you realize. I don't skulk around like a guilty person, because I've done nothing to be ashamed of. And maybe, just maybe, the more I show my face around Love, the more people will come to realize that they misjudged me."

Hearing those words tumble out of Paige's mouth caused a feeling of doubt to slither through him. Was he one of those people? After all, he was far from convinced of Paige's innocence. It was one of the main reasons he knew they could never have a future together. Trust was a cornerstone to every relationship. Without it, the foundation would crumble into dust.

He cleared his throat. "That's mighty brave of you to volunteer. And if you really want to help, I could sure use an extra pair of hands."

Paige smiled so wide he thought it might take over her entire face. "Terrific. That's great. Let me call Fiona and have her pick up Emma at the café."

At the sound of her name, Emma stretched her hands toward Paige, begging with her eyes to be back in her mother's arms. Paige plucked Emma out of his arms. Cameron immediately missed the little bundle he'd cradled. She had smelled of baby powder and lavender.

Even though Paige was helping him out in a pinch, he still wasn't certain he should have agreed to let her waitress for him. Being near her was stirring up emotions he was struggling to suppress. For so long he had convinced himself that she was nothing more than a liar and a fraud. Now, with her unexpected return, she was showing him with every word and deed how wrong he'd been. Dishonorable women didn't risk everything to return to a place that had virtually disowned them. Untrustworthy women didn't rack their brains trying to figure out a way to bring revenue to a struggling town.

As he drove away from Paige and Emma toward Jarvis Street and the Moose Café, he fought against old feelings that threatened to choke him. Against his best intentions and his resolve to remain immune to Paige, she had swarmed over him like a hive of honeybees, leaving him feeling defenseless and rattled by her presence in his world. Although he was committed to being the best possible father he could be, there was no way he was going to allow Paige back into his heart. Been there, done that. He had the bruises to prove it. He wasn't going down that road again.

The Moose Café was packed to the gills with customers. Cameron had really hit the nail on the head when he'd made the decision to open a coffee bar–eatery, Paige marveled as the hum and buzz of the lunch crowd pulsed in the air. The success of the café spoke volumes about Cameron's work ethic and his ability to tap into the needs of his beloved community. From what she had observed, they'd all given his establishment a huge stamp of approval.

Paige had felt triumph surge through her as she served her first customers of the day. Although she had received a few not-so-pleasant stares, the majority of the townsfolk simply seemed happy to be waited on. Not a single one had declined service from her. A few had even greeted her warmly by name. On occasion she'd caught Cameron staring at her. As soon as she met his gaze, he'd glanced away, making her wonder if she'd imagined his scrutiny.

She couldn't seem to wipe the grin off her face. Paige was certain Cameron didn't understand one bit of her elation about waitressing at the Moose Café. While he thought she was sure to get her feelings hurt by his patrons, she was regarding it as an opportunity to get back in the swing of things. Before her father had betrayed the town's trust, the Reynolds family had been popular in Love. She couldn't remember a time when she hadn't been treated with warmth and grace by the townsfolk. She had been considered a hometown girl, even though she hadn't been born in town. A sense of community had been what she had been missing in Seattle.

She looked down at her T-shirt. The big cartoon moose seemed to be laughing at her. No doubt he questioned the wisdom of what she was hoping to achieve here in Love. She let out a giggle, earning herself a few stares from customers. Oh, brother! As if they needed yet another reason to be suspicious of her. Now they might just suspect she was plumb crazy.

"You! Miss Paige Reynolds." Paige froze at the imperious tone of the woman's voice calling out her name. She turned her head toward the voice and saw long, weathered hands with fire-engine-red nails beckoning her. Letting out a low groan, she made her way over to the table.

"I almost cannot believe my eyes!" the woman cried out.

Paige had to bite her tongue. The Duchess, Myrtle Maplethorpe, was known for her fantastic, colorful ensembles and her snobby manner, among other things. She was a town gossip and their local historian.

"Mrs. Maplethorpe. How lovely to see you. It's been such a long time," Paige said, oozing every ounce of charm she had in her arsenal.

Myrtle peered up at her as if she were examining her for defects. She blinked furiously behind her glasses. "They said you'd come back, but I had to see it with my own eyes."

With her thick Coke-bottle glasses, she had been long-rumored to be unable to see very much of anything, although she'd had no difficulty spotting Paige. She knew from experience that what the older woman didn't see with her own eyes she made up with her fanciful imagination. It was important to tread lightly with Myrtle. The last thing she needed in this world was to be the subject of unfounded gossip. From what Paige remembered, Myrtle dished up dirt the way Cameron provided coffee drinks in the café. Hot and steaming.

She forced herself to smile. "Yes, I'm back," she said, her voice filled with false cheer. Myrtle Maplethorpe had always got under her skin. She was an uncharitable, mean-spirited woman masquerading as a paragon. Paige knew people like this were dangerous.

"And rumor has it you brought a baby back with

you," Myrtle continued in a scandalized tone. She made a tutting sound and shook her head. "I can't believe you kept that poor child separated from her father for so long." She arched an eyebrow at Paige. "If he is indeed the father."

Paige opened her mouth to tell Myrtle that she could take a flying leap off the town pier, as far as she was concerned. All of a sudden Cameron was there standing beside her. His hand reached for her arm in a familiar gesture that was meant to rein her in. "Well, hello there, Myrtle. You're looking lovely in that purple turban," Cameron gushed.

Myrtle swatted her hand in his direction. "Oh, stop your flattery. You could charm the birds right out of the trees, Cameron Prescott." She peeped out at him from over her glasses. "I was just chatting with Paige here about how shockingly she has acted in the secret-baby department. Imagine keeping something so vital from a father who hails from one of Love's founding families!"

"If I've learned anything at all about life, Myrtle, it's that things aren't always what they seem." He narrowed his gaze at her. "What really matters is that I'm the proud father of a little girl. I'm so happy about it I could do backflips."

Myrtle blinked furiously a few times. She looked back and forth between them, then cleared her throat. "I—I see. I'm rather pleased that you're stepping up to heed the call of fatherhood. Some of us might want to throw you a baby shower."

Cameron's eyes went wide and he began to stammer.

"Th-that's awfully sweet of you, Myrtle, but Emma has everything she needs."

Myrtle cut her eyes at Cameron, then looked away from him. She snapped her menu open with a flourish. "I'll have the Alaskan omelet with a side of hash browns and a coffee, black, no sugar."

Paige scribbled her order down and said in a chirpy voice, "Coming right up, hot off the griddle."

She turned on her heel and hurried toward the kitchen so she could put the order in with Magda, the new cook. According to Cameron, Magda had recently arrived in town with the hopes of finding her other half in the wilds of Alaska as a participant in Operation Love. She was tall and solid with long dark hair she wore in pigtails. And she could cook like nobody's business. After placing the order in the rotation, Paige turned around and came face-to-face with Cameron. He was eyeing her with a concerned expression etched on his face.

"Thanks for not losing your cool with Myrtle. She said some pretty offensive things, from what I overheard."

"You didn't have to step in like that. She's nothing but a busybody. I can take my lumps from Myrtle," Paige said, a hint of impatience in her voice.

Cameron knit his brow. "You shouldn't have to. None of it is any of her business, for starters. Just because she deems herself the social maven of this town doesn't mean she can barrel her way into your personal life. She's been gossiping so long I'm surprised her jaw isn't swollen shut from talking too much."

Paige snickered. She covered her mouth out of fear

she might let loose with a rip-roaring hoot of laughter. The corners of Cameron's mouth began to twitch. The sight of it caused her to chuckle even harder until she was in full-on belly-busting-laughter mode. She clutched her stomach as waves of mirth rolled through her. The more she thought about Myrtle with her purple turban and her thick glasses, the more she couldn't stop herself from giggling. The idea of her being unable to speak was downright hilarious.

Hazel strode into the back hallway, stopping short when she caught sight of them. She threw her hands on her hips. "Sorry to break up this laughathon, but we've got hungry customers out there," Hazel barked.

Paige swiped at her eyes with the back of her hand while Cameron straightened his posture and took a calming breath. Hazel looked back and forth between the two of them. She shook her head, then walked toward the kitchen with a few order slips in her hand.

"We should get back out there," Cameron said in a bemused voice. His lips were still twitching with merriment.

"We should," Paige agreed, wishing this lighthearted moment between them could stretch for a bit longer. This was the first time in a very long while that she'd felt as if the parts of Cameron she had always loved best still existed. He wasn't as humorless and somber as he appeared to be. He wasn't all doubts and frowns. There was still a lightness and a humor inside him. It hadn't been destroyed by her father's betrayal and lies. Despite all he'd been through and the hard shell he wore as a defense mechanism, he was still the man she had fallen in love with all those years ago.

Ever since she was seventeen years old, she had worn her heart on her sleeve when it came to Cameron Prescott. Those days were over. All it had got her was pain, betrayal and disillusionment. It hurt her to remember how he had once meant the world to her. She missed being in love with someone. And even though it felt nice to be sharing a sweet moment, she couldn't allow herself to forget that loving him had already shredded her to pieces once before. She was determined to never let it happen again.

Cameron spent the rest of the afternoon forcing himself not to stare at Paige as she took orders, serviced customers and hustled back and forth to the kitchen. She was handling the current situation with such grace and integrity. Several times he'd wanted to intervene when a customer had a few choice words for her. In each and every instance Paige had found the perfect words to defuse the situation. She'd been humble and genuine in addressing the sins of her father, while making it clear she didn't intend to be criticized for his actions.

Paige seemed incredibly sincere. Had he misjudged her?

"What's wrong with you?" Hazel asked as she walked past him with a tray of used plates and utensils. "You look like the sky is falling."

"Nothing." He shook his head, hoping to shake off all his worries. He threw his hands up in the air as a feeling of helplessness washed over him. For two years he had worked so hard to get his life in order. Now it felt as if everything was out of his control. Paige was making him question whether he had been on the wrong side of things when she was deemed guilty by the town. "The truth is, Paige's return is reminding me of everything I lost when she left Love. And just when I thought my life was getting back on track, now I find myself scratching my head about the future. I suddenly have a daughter that needs to take center stage in my life." He brushed his hand over his face. "Things in my world are suddenly more complicated than ever."

"Life is complicated," Hazel said. "The good Lord never promised us a cakewalk."

"You've got that right. I grew up hearing Jasper say that you have to walk through the valley to get to the mountaintop. Don't tell him I said so, but now more than ever I'm learning to appreciate his wisdom."

Hazel cackled. "I won't tell him. My honey muffin already has a slight ego. No need to inflate it like a balloon." She patted Cameron on the arm. "Keep in mind that sometimes the things that bless us the most are the ones that come straight out of the blue without any warning." She beamed at him. "Like that precious child of yours."

Cameron grinned at the thought of his daughter. Hazel was right to remind him of the blessing. Emma was just about as perfect as one could imagine. Innocent. Full of hope and promise. He never wanted her to suffer even the slightest bit for the choices he and Paige had made. He wanted her to rise and soar like an eagle. And he needed to make it clear to Paige that he was committed to doing whatever it took to give Emma the life she deserved.

"Why, if it isn't the most gorgeous woman who ever lived and breathed." The loud voice carried through the café like a foghorn. Cameron didn't even have to glance over to know who had come barreling into his establishment. Declan O'Rourke was like clockwork. Pretty much the same time every day, he came in for an afternoon latte. More times than not, Boone joined him.

"Declan!" Paige cried out. Cameron watched from across the room as Declan leaned down for a hug and wrapped Paige up in his long arms, then spun her around for good measure. Cameron felt a wild urge to punch him in the nose. Declan might have been Boone's best friend and a lifelong pal, but the sight of him hugging Paige felt like being doused with a bucket of ice-cold water. At six foot two, with a head of blond hair and movie-star good looks, Declan had always been the golden boy. The one most likely to make ladies' hearts flutter. He was also an honorary member of the Prescott family.

Declan had never made a secret of his affection for Paige. He'd always flirted shamelessly with her. Back when Paige was Cameron's girlfriend, it hadn't bothered him, since he'd never doubted her devotion to him. Now Declan threatened to make him lose every ounce of composure he still had.

With a sour feeling in his gut, he turned away from the sight of them, focusing instead on the lunch specials for the rest of the week. Even though he was trying to concentrate on the menu, all he could hear was the loud drone of Declan's voice.

Before he knew it, Boone had sidled up to him. "You know it doesn't mean anything. He's just being Declan. He was flirting with pretty girls back in kindergarten."

Cameron shrugged. "I don't have a claim on Paige. If Declan wants to chase after her, that's his business."

Boone folded his arms across his chest and rocked back on his heels. "He's not exactly chasing after her, Cameron. They're simply catching up on old times."

"What part of *I don't care* don't you understand?" he spit out. Boone was buzzing around him like a gnat at the moment, serving no other purpose than to annoy him.

Boone grunted. "You can try to sell that story somewhere else, little brother—to someone who hasn't known you your entire life."

Cameron turned his head to look at Boone. "What do you want me to say? That I feel like walking over there and knocking his teeth out?"

Boone narrowed his gaze. "I don't need you to say anything. Just listen for a second. I almost lost Gracie due to false pride and not wanting to take a chance at loving again." He shook his head, a fierce expression stamped on his face. "Take a lesson from me. If you still love Paige, don't waste another minute rehashing the past or creating problems where there aren't any. Do it for Emma. Show her the power that exists when two people commit themselves to one another for life."

"It's not that simple," Cameron said. He cast a quick glance over at Paige. Her head was thrown back in merriment as she laughed at something Declan had said to her. She looked relaxed and happy. A tight feeling settled over his chest. He couldn't remember the last time he had been able to make her feel that way.

Boone followed the path of his gaze. "And why not?"

"I loved Paige years ago, but a lot of water has flowed under that bridge. I'm sure you remember that when she left town, it wasn't of her own accord."

"I remember," Boone said with a solemn nod. "She was practically run out on a rail."

Cameron swung his gaze back toward his brother. "I was the one who gave her the final push to leave. There were a lot of things that had me convinced she was in collusion with her father. Things I haven't been able to forget. Big-ticket items she purchased, trips, jewelry. All of which I suspect she couldn't have afforded on her salary."

"None of which is concrete proof of her guilt," Boone said. "I'll admit I had suspicions in the past about Paige, but after seeing her desire to make things right here in town and your beautiful little girl, it's forced me to reflect on things. God placed her right in your path again. From where I'm standing, it looks like you have another shot to get it right."

"It's not as if we can just pick up where we left off. Because of everything that took place two years ago, I lost fourteen months of my daughter's life. Pushing Paige out of town had consequences. Every time I look at Paige, I'm consumed by so much guilt and regret. I need some time to process all of these feelings."

Boone clapped him on the shoulder. "You're a good

man. Don't beat yourself up about it. Wallowing in the past won't move you toward your future."

His future. He didn't know exactly what that meant. No doubt it would be full of diapers and sippy cups and all kinds of girlie things he had no clue about. Taffeta and lace. Pink teddy bears and tiaras. Dolls and tea parties. He pressed his eyes closed as anxiety gnawed at him. Was he up for the challenges of fatherhood? He was coming at it late in the game. He wasn't so sure it would be easy to play catch-up.

He still hadn't discussed any specifics with Paige. Would Emma be growing up here in Love or back in Seattle? Was he going to be raising his daughter long-distance or sharing custody with Paige? His heart ached at the thought of how confusing two households in different states would be. His own parents' divorce had shattered his childhood, and when his mother had left Alaska for greener pastures, it had left a hole inside him that nothing or no one had ever been able to fill. Throw in a father who had rambled all over the world, only returning home when it suited him, and the situation had amounted to nothing more than a fine mess.

His own life had been shaped by parental abandonment. He'd struggled for so many years with feelings of loss and unworthiness. The thought of making Emma experience those same emotions gutted him. And he knew a part of him resented Paige for creating another loss in his life.

"Truth is, everything feels like it's crashing down on me at once. It's not like there's a road map pointing me in a specific direction," he admitted.

Boone made a tutting sound. "If you don't see the possibilities, I'm afraid you're going to blow this opportunity to smithereens."

"Opportunity for what? I'm a little skeptical about happily-ever-afters," he scoffed. "Our parents didn't exactly give us a lot of hope for one."

Boone clucked his tongue. "If you have to ask that question, something tells me you're not ready yet to embrace the big picture." Boone pointed his chin in Paige's direction. "Just don't wait too long to decide what you want. In a town with a shortage of women, there are plenty of men here in Love who won't hesitate to court Paige."

After shooting him a pointed look, Boone ambled off to join Declan at his table. Cameron shook his head at his brother's retreating figure. Since Boone was now ecstatically in love and married to his one and only, it was easy for him to dole out relationship advice. Boone was viewing things through rose-colored glasses. He wasn't acknowledging all of the very real obstacles that stood between him and Paige. How could he forge something new with Paige when he still questioned her role in the embezzlement that had rocked his hometown? And it was no small issue that she had kept his daughter's existence from him for all this time.

Cameron wished he still believed in things like white picket fences and dream houses with views of the mountains. He wished that things weren't so complicated with the only woman he had ever loved. A life without Paige had already proved to be a life with less color and zest. Making it through these past two years without her had brought him to his knees. He had emerged on the other side, but surely not a better man than the one who had loved so gloriously. And been loved in return.

He wasn't sure that he and Paige could ever get there again. Not when their past had been littered with so much friction and lying and judgment. Sometimes it was best to accept things the way they were and move on. Maybe this was one of those occasions, he realized.

And that knowledge was all kinds of heartbreaking to him.

Chapter Six

Paige smiled at the group of women who were seated at a large table by the window. There were six of them in all, and from what she'd gathered of their conversation, they were all participants in the Operation Love program. The women had come from Maine, Louisiana, Texas and Idaho to find love and companionship with the single bachelors in Love.

Paige placed a basketful of blueberry muffins and scones down on the table, along with a pot of hot water and an assortment of teas. The ladies smiled at her and murmured a round of thank-yous.

The one named Gretchen darted a glance behind Paige. "There he is. He's the most handsome man in this whole town." Gretchen put her elbow on the table, then placed her jaw on her hand so she could stare moon-eyed into the distance.

"And he owns this café," the dark-haired woman with glasses chimed in.

"Why do you think I suggested having tea here?

Great food and an even greater view," Gretchen said. All the women giggled.

Cameron! Of course they had their eye on him. After all, he was a single, gorgeous Alaskan male. A hottie, according to the ladies. Paige's chest tightened. Her cheeks suddenly felt warm. She fought against a sudden urge to tell the women to back off. The feeling terrified her since she had no claim on Cameron. Sure, he was Emma's father, but he was no longer hers. She had no right to be upset, although her out-of-control pulse hadn't quite got the message.

"And what about that pilot with the killer smile?" another of the ladies asked. "I couldn't take my eyes off him."

"Go for it, Dahlia. He's single, unlike that rugged-looking sheriff. I heard he just got married a few months ago to a journalist who came here to write a story about Operation Love," Gretchen said with a knowing look. "See, ladies. There really are happily-ever-afters in this town."

Paige walked away from the table with the empty tray in her hands and an unsettled feeling in the pit of her stomach. She knew she had no right to feel territorial about Cameron, but the thought of him settling down with one of these women bothered her deeply. The emotions traveled all the way down to her gut. She wasn't in love with him anymore, so why did she care so much?

Feeling on edge, she walked back toward the kitchen as she battled against a huge, gnawing feeling in her belly. Rather than dwell on the jealousy eating up her insides, she wanted to focus on something positive. Running into Declan had been a nice surprise. To be greeted so warmly by a friend here in Love restored her hope that one day the townsfolk might view her in a better light. If he was to be believed, she had been missed by many of the villagers.

"Declan seemed mighty glad to see you," Cameron said, quirking his mouth.

"He hasn't changed one bit," Paige said with a chuckle. "He's something else."

"That's for sure," Cameron muttered. He set a cup down on the counter with a bang.

She couldn't miss the big frown on Cameron's face and the fact that he was being short with her. His tone was sharp. After such a nice day when they had actually enjoyed some light moments together, it felt like a slap in the face. Yet another rejection from Cameron. They were back to square one. What had she done? Or had Cameron just remembered that he neither liked nor trusted her?

Paige let out a wounded sigh. She had volunteered to work at the café today because she wanted to put her best foot forward and show Cameron that she could pitch in and help out when needed. Even if he didn't realize it, she was still part of the fabric of this town. But it didn't matter, she supposed. No one seemed to recognize that fact but her.

Would she always be considered guilty by association?

"Why don't you sit down for a bowl of salmon chowder? You've been on your feet for hours." Unbeknownst to her, Cameron had walked up behind her. His voice was full of a gentleness that caught her by surprise.

Salmon chowder? Although she would have liked to turn Cameron's offer down and leave in a huff, her stomach was growling like a grizzly bear. She had sat down earlier for a grilled vegetable sandwich, but things had been so hectic that she'd barely swallowed a few bites. From what she had observed in the kitchen, Cameron had created an impeccable menu for his establishment. He'd really knocked it out of the park by combining coffee and culinary items such as reindeer pizza, homemade baked goods and mouthwatering sandwiches.

Before she knew it, Cameron had pulled out a chair for her and motioned her to sit down. Paige nodded her head and sat down.

A few seconds later Hazel came to sit beside her. She let out a grunt. "Oh, these dogs are killing me." She swung her booted feet up onto the chair across from her. "These bones of mine are aching something fierce. Enjoy your youth while you can."

Paige paused to admire Hazel's boots. "I remember when those boots were a twinkle in your eye. I'm real proud of you for going the distance and producing them. It sounds like you're about to make a big splash."

Hazel threw her arms heavenward. "Can you believe it? You could have knocked me over with a feather when Grace suggested that we mass-produce my boots as a way of earning revenue for the town. Now everyone is all fired up about it. God's favor is what I call it."

"Love is blessed to have you," Paige said.

"That's mighty kind of you to say, considering the way I treated you," Hazel said, blinking away tears. "I'm ashamed that I didn't support you when you needed me. We just all felt so betrayed by Robert. He was a friend of this town. Beloved by all. I'm not trying to hurt your feelings, but it was such a terrible blow. Can't say if we've ever fully recovered from it."

Paige reached across the table and squeezed Hazel's hands. "I know how hard hit this town was by what my father did. And I know I can never fully make amends for what happened, but I want to try to make things better. Not just because he asked me to, but for Emma. So she can hold her head up high in this town."

"Emma will never have a problem being accepted in Love. I'll see to that," Cameron said as he put two bowls of salmon chowder down in front of them. He placed a basket of piping-hot bread in the middle of the table along with two root beers. The smell of the bread was so delectable she felt like kissing Cameron for bringing it to them.

Paige looked up and met his intense gaze. She knew without a doubt that his word was bond. She smiled at him, feeling secure in the knowledge that he would always make sure Emma was protected and loved in this town.

Cameron smiled back at her. Even though she tried to keep her cool, it did funny things to her insides. She felt like a giddy schoolgirl. Cameron turned right around and headed back toward the kitchen with the empty tray.

Hazel sent her a questioning look.

Paige shrugged. "When Cameron smiles, he's pretty

irresistible. He gives me mixed signals, though. One moment he's grinning, while the next he's a bear. It was easier when I left town and he didn't care at all about it. At least then I knew where things stood between us."

"Didn't care?" Hazel sputtered. "If that man had cared any more, he'd be six feet under."

Six feet under? "Wh-what are you talking about?"

Hazel let out a huff of air. "Say what you will about Cameron, but when he loves, he loves hard. Losing you was like losing a limb, Paige. He wasn't eating or sleeping or living in the first few weeks after you left. If you ever tell him I told you, I'll deny it, but in the beginning he was so torn up he could barely get out of bed."

Paige felt as if the wind had been knocked out of her. Cameron had cut off all communication with her following her departure. After a while she'd stopped trying to reach out to him, knowing her messages were falling on deaf ears. It hurt terribly to discover that he had been as devastated as she had been by their breakup. They had both suffered. And for what? False allegations that had destroyed what could have been a loving family—herself, Cameron and Emma. It was devastating to consider the ripples of the rumors and innuendos lodged against her. And Cameron's betrayal still sat wedged in her chest. He hadn't once apologized for pushing her out of town. Matter of fact, she had the feeling that he still believed in her guilt.

What had made her fall under the town's suspicions in the first place? Her close relationship with her father? The fact that she hadn't been born and bred in Love? Small towns could be funny about those they viewed as newcomers as opposed to the locals who had taken their first breaths in Love. It was so frustrating to know that her entire destiny had been shaped by a big huge misconception.

She set her spoon down with a clang. "I'm sorry he suffered, Hazel, but he wasn't the only one. To this day, I have no idea why he turned against me other than that he was influenced by the townsfolk."

Hazel paused in eating her soup. "I didn't mean to ruffle your feathers. I just couldn't let you sit here and say that Cameron didn't care when I know for a fact he did. And the only one who has answers to that question is Cameron himself."

They continued to eat in silence until Hazel pushed back from her chair and stood up.

"Well, I'm going to head on out. I'm supposed to be meeting up with Jasper at the mayor's office. You leaving, too?"

"I'll be going home in a few minutes. First there's a few things I'd like to discuss with Cameron." Her expression must have said it all, since Hazel nodded, picked up her bowl and went toward the kitchen as though her feet were on fire. She must have exited the back way, since she didn't make another appearance in the dining area. Paige grunted. Perhaps she was in the kitchen warning Cameron that she was stewing for a talk. Hazel and Cameron were as thick as thieves. More like mother and son than anything.

For the life of her she couldn't stop thinking about all the unanswered questions she had for Cameron. It just wasn't right to sandbag someone's life and never be held accountable.

According to what Hazel had revealed, they had both been suffering broken hearts at the same time. And for what? Cameron's erroneous belief that she'd somehow been tied up in her father's schemes? She felt a swell of anger rise over her. It was an emotion she had tried so hard to bury. Anger didn't allow a person to move forward. She had never wanted to be one of those mothers who was so caught up in bitterness that she allowed it to affect her child. Emma deserved a happy life full of grace and harmony.

Forgiving Cameron for his blindness had been an important step in building a new life. It didn't mean she had forgotten that he had turned his back on her in her time of need. His actions had let her know in no uncertain terms that any future between them was unthinkable. How could she ever put her faith in a man who had blindsided her in such cruel fashion? Being back in Love and facing Cameron was causing all sorts of emotions to rise to the surface.

And now, with all this fury building up inside her like a slow-burning fire, she needed to snuff it out. And there was only one way to do that. By putting Cameron on the spot and asking him the specifics about two years ago. In order to fully get closure on the whole situation, she needed answers.

The heavy tread of Cameron's footsteps interrupted her thoughts. He was standing next to the table, looking at her with a quizzical expression. "What happened to Hazel? She blew out of here like a Category 3 hurricane," he said with a tilt of his head.

"I think she knew I wanted to talk to you and she didn't want to get caught in the cross fire."

Cameron narrowed his gaze. "Cross fire? Sounds serious."

"It is serious. To me."

She stood up from the table and walked in his direction, quickly swallowing up the space between them. They needed to be on equal footing for this discussion.

He was standing there with his arms folded across his chest. She had to look up at him, and that immediately made her feel vulnerable. He was tall and imposing. She suddenly wished that she were a whole lot taller than her five feet seven inches. She folded her arms around her middle and jutted her chin at him. Her body bristled with fury.

"So tell me, Cameron. What exactly did I do to make you doubt me? To make you believe I could actually steal from this town and sandbag the cannery deal? To cause you to run me out of town? After all this time, I think I deserve some answers."

Cameron knew a moment of reckoning when it was staring him straight in the face. The fiery glint in Paige's hazel eyes served as a warning that she wouldn't be satisfied with mere platitudes.

What could he say to justify his actions? That she had appeared guilty? That he had been easily swayed by town sentiment? No. That made it sound as if he hadn't harbored suspicions on his own. He wasn't going to throw the town under the bus. The truth was his only option.

"When I found out about Robert's embezzlement of the funds, I was blindsided. And completely and utterly devastated. It broke me." Tears pricked his eyes. "Your father was my mentor and one of my closest friends. In many ways he was a father figure to me, especially since my own father has been in and out of my life so much. I thought he pretty much hung the moon." He couldn't stop his voice from trembling with emotion. This was the stuff he kept hidden away from the world. The raw emotions that were tied in to loss, betrayal and abandonment. Robert Reynolds's betrayal hadn't been just a matter of dollars and cents. It had been deeply personal.

"Because I worked so closely with him on the project, all eyes turned to me when he disappeared. What did I know? When did I know it? Was I involved in the scheme? Was my girlfriend in on it? And then your name started to get tossed around. Everyone in town knew what a close relationship the two of you shared. It was almost inconceivable to think that you weren't aware of what was going on. You shared a home. He was your best friend."

"No, Cameron," Paige interrupted. "He wasn't my best friend. You were."

Her words sliced through him like a knife. He actually felt a physical pain in his side. Yes. Paige was right. Part of the beauty of their relationship had been the tight friendship they had shared even before the romance had ever started. He took a deep, steadying breath. Even though hashing things out was painful, he had to get it all out. He had to tell her everything. After two years he needed to be straight with her.

He cleared his throat. "The truth is, I kept thinking about all the purchases you had made around that time. You were only working part-time as a consultant, but it seemed as if you were flush with money. The new car. A host of new outfits. Jewelry. The Hawaii trip."

Paige winced. She shook her head. "I can't believe you thought I used stolen funds. I received money from my mother's estate, Cameron. It was turned over to me on my twenty-fifth birthday. And I plan to turn it over to Emma on her twenty-first birthday so she'll have a nest egg. I was a little foolish with some of the money at the time, but it was mine to use."

Bile rose in his throat. Paige had never divulged to him that she had money from a trust fund.

"It also seemed incredible to me that you had no idea where he'd gone when he disappeared from Love. Or that he hadn't reached out to you," Cameron added. He let out a huge shudder. "As much as Robert adored you, it just seemed impossible to believe that you didn't have those answers. It felt like you were hiding things from us so we couldn't pursue legal action against him. Or that you had planned to meet up with him the whole time."

Tears slid down Paige's face and he resisted the urge to brush them away. Honesty came at a price, he realized. He'd hurt Paige by giving her the truthful answers she'd been seeking. All he wanted to do in this moment was take her into his arms and hold her against his chest to soothe her tears. He took a halting step forward, then stopped.

Did he still have the right to comfort her?

"But I didn't know his whereabouts. I promise you. He told me nothing," Paige insisted. "It wasn't until months later that he showed up in Seattle telling me he had only a few months to live. I took him in because he was sick and dying and remorseful. No matter what he had done, I forgave him in that moment. I extended grace to him, knowing his life was ebbing away with every breath he took. So if I'm guilty of anything, it's that. For giving my father a place to stay and for taking care of him instead of turning him in to the authorities. I admit that I did those things."

Years ago, even months ago, he would have felt scornful about Paige's explanation for harboring her father. But now, after holding his own daughter in his arms, all he felt was compassion. For a daughter who had a generous heart and a man who knew his time in this world had been coming to an end. And what an end it had been for Robert. Ravaged by cancer and vilified for being a thief and a liar. He wouldn't wish that kind of downfall on any human being, especially not a man who had taught him so much about life.

"I can't fault you for loving your father," Cameron blurted out. "I'm glad you could provide him comfort in his final weeks."

Paige's eyes widened. She wasn't the only one shocked by his statement. He'd managed to surprise himself with the admission. Mere days ago he wouldn't have been able to say these words. His resentment toward Robert and Paige had been too strong and too ingrained in his very being.

Once Paige had stepped foot back in Love with his daughter, something had shifted inside him. Talking to Boone earlier had cemented it. Paige might very well be innocent. He was no longer certain of her culpability. Two years ago there had been such a frenzy over Robert Reynolds and the embezzled money that everyone in Love had wanted to place blame. Paige had been the perfect scapegoat. He had to own his part in it. Rather than shout down the accusations, he had been so twisted up inside by Robert's betrayal that he'd allowed himself to believe in Paige's guilt. And he realized now that she had paid the ultimate price for her father's crimes.

"Since you came back, I've been racking my brain trying to figure things out. It shames me to admit that I made assumptions about you, Paige. You were as much a victim as everybody else in this town. Maybe even more. You were driven out of your hometown based on suspicions and accusations. Because of what happened, you lost faith in your father. And that's a terrible thing. I've been down that road myself with both my parents. I know what a kick in the gut it is."

"I wish that I could say I understand completely, but I don't," Paige said in a low voice. "We loved each other. You were the other half of me. How could you have forgotten what we meant to each other?"

Cameron clenched his teeth. "I didn't forget. I've never forgotten. Not then. Not now. I allowed my suspicions and anger to color my view of things. I'll have to live with my colossal mistake, and someday I'll have to explain it to Emma."

Paige's chin trembled. She looked down and fumbled with her fingers. "I wasn't treated fairly by you or this town. I'm glad you are able to acknowledge that you were wrong. I hope one day soon the town will be able to recognize that I was innocent of wrongdoing. I want that for myself, but also for our daughter."

Cameron had no idea if the townsfolk were at a point where they could see the error in their judgment of her. After believing Paige to be guilty for so long, it felt a little strange to let it all go. But, he had to admit, he felt as if a mighty weight had been lifted from his shoulders.

"For the time being I think we should focus on Emma and your idea for the cannery," he suggested.

Paige nodded. "I agree. It would be wonderful if everyone in town rallies around moving forward with that project."

Cameron couldn't help but chuckle. So far Paige was proving to be very determined in her quest. As far as she was concerned, all roads led back to the cannery.

"What's so funny?" she asked, a slight scowl marring her stunning features.

How had he forgotten that Paige hated to be laughed at? It was a pet peeve of hers that went all the way back to her teenage years.

He held up his hands. "I'm not laughing at you, but your persistence reminds me of that feisty fifteen-year-old girl who wouldn't rest until Love declared a special day for snowy owls."

Paige let out a low chuckle that seemed to emanate

from deep inside her. She raised her hand to her mouth as if self-conscious. "I thought they deserved some recognition. They are unbelievably beautiful and underappreciated."

Cameron grinned as memories of Paige's snowy-owl campaign trickled through his mind. She had been full of passion and grit and dedication. And her efforts had paid off. To this day, the town had an annual "show some love to snowy owls" day. All thanks to Paige. It served as a reminder that this woman was capable of making incredible things happen by sheer will and determination. For the first time since she'd brought up the topic, he was beginning to believe that the cannery project might actually get off the ground.

"I've always loved snowy owls. I still do. And so does your daughter."

Your daughter. The shock in hearing those words was beginning to wear off. All he felt now was a fierce desire to get to know Emma.

"In a few weeks they'll be back in Alaska for breeding season. Maybe Emma would like to go out to the Nottingham Woods and catch a glimpse of them."

Paige nodded. The corners of her lips turned upward into a radiant smile that traveled straight through him. "That would be great. I know she would be pleased with any kind of outing."

"I want to get to know her. Her favorite color. What she likes to eat. The things that make her cry." He felt a pang at the realization that he didn't know very much about his own daughter. All he knew for certain was that he wanted to discover every last fact about her. Her birthday. Did she like puppies?

"Forgive me for robbing you of those answers," Paige said. Her hazel eyes were full of regret. "If I'd told you about Emma sooner, you'd already know all those things. For starters, Emma loves pink. And her birthday is December 5th. The sound of thunder makes her cry. And she loves pancakes."

He couldn't dwell on all the lost moments. All he could do was focus on what lay ahead. Hopefully, a lifetime as Emma's dutiful, doting father.

The old has passed away; behold, the new has come. The verse from Corinthians served as reassurance of the path he was walking on. There was no more time for holding on to bitterness.

"I think it's safe to say that we both want what's beneficial for Emma. The best way to give her that is to give ourselves a clean slate with each other. We need to put the past firmly behind us." And in doing so, they would be cementing a bright and happy future for their child. Recriminations would only serve to hurt her. His own childhood living under the roof of two feuding parents had caused him more pain than he could ever adequately express with words. Emma's life would not be marred by friction and discord.

Paige released a huge breath. Her features appeared less tense than a few moments ago.

"I think I can live with that," she said with a nod of her head.

On impulse, he reached out and brushed her hair away from her face. His fingers trailed down her cheek, lingering way longer than they should have. Their eyes held and locked. Tension simmered in the air between them. He took a step closer so that they stood mere inches away from each other. His finger moved toward her lips and he gently traced the outline of them. If he just dipped his head down, their lips could meet in the sweetest of kisses. Just one tender caress might serve as a reminder of everything they had once shared.

The familiar jingle of a bell warned him that they were no longer alone, despite the Closed sign on the front door. A quick turn of his head confirmed that fact.

Paige's nanny had just crossed the threshold with Emma, who was holding her hand and taking dainty steps beside her. A brown teddy bear, who looked as if he had seen better days, was in her other hand. Although Cameron was tickled at the sight of his daughter teetering toward them, he wished his tender moment with Paige could have lasted longer. He wasn't sure if he would have followed through with it, but the sudden urge to place a soft kiss on her lips had roared through him just as they had been interrupted.

"Mama," Emma cried out, lifting her hands up to Paige. The teddy bear fell to the floor. He quickly picked it up and dusted it off on his shirt, then handed it back to Emma, who was now peeping up at him from Paige's arms.

"Here you go, princess," Cameron said in a sing-song voice.

"Say 'Thank you, Dada,'" Paige instructed. "Dada picked up Lola Bear."

Emma frowned at her mother. She shook the bear. "Lola," she repeated.

"Dada," Paige said again, then looked at Cameron. "That's Dada."

Emma looked away, then burrowed her face into Paige's chest. Cameron felt a stab of disappointment. At the moment he would give anything to hear Emma call him Daddy. It was amazing how quickly one's priorities changed once a child came into existence. But he needed to be patient. Children learned at their own time and pace. Such things couldn't be rushed.

"The wee one is plumb tuckered out. She had a fitful nap earlier," Fiona explained, stepping forward to pat Emma on the back. Paige swayed from side to side, rocking Emma into slumber.

Cameron found himself transfixed by the sight of mother and daughter sharing such a heartwarming moment. Even though he and Paige were no longer romantically involved, they were still a family.

"I should get her home," Paige whispered after a few minutes, reaching for her purse.

With a lump in his throat, Cameron said his goodbyes and watched as Paige, Emma and Fiona left the café and headed back to the homestead for the afternoon.

He didn't quite know how to explain the ache in his chest. It was as if their absence had somehow created a hole inside him that nothing else could fill up. A few days ago the Moose Café and the Prescott family had been the most important things in his world. That was no longer true. As soon as Paige had introduced him to his beautiful little girl, a portion of his heart had no longer been his own. Emma now owned a huge chunk of it. And he had the sneaking suspicion that if he wasn't careful, her mother might soon lay claim to the rest of it.

Chapter Seven

The weekly meeting for the town of Love was scheduled to start at 6:00 p.m. sharp. As Paige walked down Jarvis Street toward the historic town hall building, she took a few soothing breaths to calm her nerves. Sunlight danced across her face and she found herself feeling thankful for the extended hours of daylight. She couldn't believe Wednesday had rolled around so quickly. Doubts were beginning to creep in. Was it really a good idea to stand before the council and the residents of Love to lobby for the town to revisit the cannery deal?

Don't bite off more than you can chew, Paige. That had always been one of her father's favorite expressions. Ever since she was a little girl, he had warned her against it. More times than not, due to her stubborn nature, she hadn't heeded his advice. She stood still for a moment and shut her eyes as bittersweet memories washed over her. Her father's presence was strong in her heart and mind today. The terrible ache of loss was still there, serving as a reminder that the imperfections of human beings didn't mean they were loved any less. Hate the sin and not the sinner.

Keep going. Don't give up now. His encouraging voice whispered in the wind. Despite everything, she still was holding on to all the good qualities of the man she'd cared for so dearly. Living beyond his means had led him to do a despicable and desperate act. But it couldn't erase all the good years when he had been her everything. Now it was time for her to work toward allowing him to rest in peace.

Before she knew it, she had reached the town hall. The brick-and-white building was three stories high and one of the oldest landmarks in town. Old-fashioned lampposts graced the sidewalk in front of the building, while Arctic willow shrubs sat by the first-floor windows. Once she stepped inside, gleaming hardwood floors and copper accents jumped out at her. Steeped in history, this building was one of the most ornate in town. A hum of activity emanated from the meeting room down the hall. In order to get to the room, she had to walk the gauntlet of residents who were gathered in the hallway. Some nodded or sent a smile her way, while others began whispering or looked away at the sight of her. The murmurs were a glaring reminder that her reputation in Love was tainted by past events. Even Cameron didn't fully believe in her. Not in the ways that mattered most.

Lord, please be with me. This meeting is so important for Love's future. And it would be a huge step forward in providing closure for everyone who was harmed by my father's greed. Let their minds be open to what I have to say.

Cameron was already seated in the front row when she walked in. She let out the breath she had been holding ever since she had walked into the building. Some of his earlier comments had led her to believe he might stay away tonight. Part of her wouldn't have blamed him if he had. The first cannery project had brought him more grief and shame than he could ever have anticipated. And he still questioned whether she had been in collusion with her father. She could see the doubts radiating from his eyes now and again.

As if he sensed that she was there, Cameron turned and waved at her, beckoning her over to sit with him.

"I didn't know if you would be here," she said once she reached his side, feeling immensely relieved by his strong presence. At the moment she desperately needed to be bolstered.

"I told you I'd come. Despite what I said about not being your ally, I stand behind your proposal. And I won't hesitate to let folks in town know that I think it's a no-brainer."

Gratitude swelled inside her chest. "Thank you. That makes me feel so much better. My nerves are beginning to get the best of me." She smoothed back a few runaway strands of hair.

Cameron gazed down at her, his handsome features creased with concern.

"Remember what brought you back. Emma and your father's dying wish. You're acting in the best interests of this town. Don't overthink this. I don't think you can go wrong if you speak from your heart."

She smiled at him. He was such a great support system. Memories of the sweet relationship they had once shared filled her head. "You're right about that. I just have to keep in mind what I'm fighting for by coming here and advocating for the cannery."

"And don't forget to mention that huge check you gave to Jasper. That's sure to win over hearts and minds," Cameron said with an easy smile that made its way up to his eyes.

It felt wonderful to have his encouragement, but she didn't want to rely on him too much for emotional support. It would be so easy to give in to the familiar rhythms of their past relationship. Those days were gone forever! For Emma's sake they had agreed to work together and stay positive, but being around Cameron was dangerous to Paige's equilibrium. She had promised herself she'd view him as the father of her child and nothing more. But that was becoming more and more of a problem. The other day at the Moose Café she had yearned for a kiss from him. When he had moved close to her and touched her lips, she had sensed it was coming. In that moment she had wanted it more than anything else in the world.

And she still did. Even now, in the midst of this important meeting, she still couldn't stop thinking about reliving that moment with Cameron. And it was distracting her from the matter at hand.

As six o'clock approached, she watched as Jasper, Boone and Hazel took their seats along with the other members of the town council. Townsfolk began spilling into the room until it was standing room only.

Cameron leaned toward her and whispered, "Standing room only. You don't see that very often here."

Something told her that word had got out about her appearance here tonight. It seemed highly unlikely that a town meeting would be overflowing with so many people.

Jasper called them all to order and promptly began to go over the minutes from the last meeting. She sat through dry discussions about town ordinances, zoning issues, business permits and a complicated issue about a runaway moose. It was all so terribly uninteresting, she realized. Paige perked up when Jasper began to give the stats for the Operation Love program.

Jasper reached for his glasses and perched them on the bridge of his nose. "Let's see. According to my records, forty-four women have arrived after the story broke about Gracie and Boone's romance. That media blitz gave this town a lot of mileage." Jasper chuckled and darted a glance in Boone's direction. "It seems that everyone is inspired by an old-fashioned love story." A smattering of applause rang out in the room.

"So far we have a grand total of sixty-six women who decided to relocate here in the pursuit of love," Jasper announced. "I think that deserves a hearty round of applause." A heavy thunder of applause ensued.

"How many decided not to stay?" someone called out from the audience.

"I was getting to that! Haven't you ever heard that patience is a virtue?" Jasper barked. He looked down at his folder. "A total of seventeen of these ladies decided they couldn't hack it in Alaska."

"Is there any indication as to why these women chose not to stay in Love?" Boone asked. "Perhaps if we find those answers, we can head off any issues that might arise."

Jasper frowned at Boone, who was sitting on his right side. "If someone comes to this haven and makes the foolish decision to leave, I'm not going to pepper them with questions about the whys and wherefores. It takes strength of character to live in an Alaskan fishing village. We should just look at it as weeding out the weak ones."

Cameron let out a groan at Jasper's comment. He put his head in his hands.

"That leaves a total of forty-nine plucky and admirable ladies for you fortunate single men who are seeking the woman of your dreams. And thanks to Hazel, most of them are living at Black Bear Cabins." He peered out into the audience. "I don't know what some of you men are waiting for. Do you need an engraved invitation to go courting? I'm talking to you, Ricky Stanton. And you, Hank Jeffries. Don't think I don't see you in the back row, Declan O'Rourke. You're known as the most handsome man in town, according to what the females say. Don't you think it's high time you settled down with a good woman? You've got almost fifty to choose from."

"Sure thing, Jasper," Declan drawled. "I'll get right on that."

"Jasper. Stop poking at Declan," Hazel said in a loud stage whisper from his left side. "Get on with it."

He shuffled his papers. "And now I have some news that involves town finances."

Dwight Lewis, town treasurer, piped up. "Finances? Isn't that under my purview?"

"Don't get yourself in a snit," Jasper said. "This financial matter falls under the heading of special circumstances. I reserve my rights and privileges as town mayor to address it in any manner I see fit."

Dwight nodded his head but he didn't appear mollified by Jasper's explanation. Having gone to high school with Dwight, Paige knew he had a bent for order and following the rules without exception. She could sense by the way he was fiddling with his bow tie that he was unsettled by Jasper encroaching on his job description.

"As part of this exciting news, I need to shine a spotlight on one of our own, a native daughter of this village." He swung his gaze to Paige. "Some of you might have heard that Paige Reynolds is back in town." A low rumble went up in the room. A few hisses rent the air. Her cheeks burned with embarrassment.

"Hush!" Jasper said. He raised his gavel and banged it on the table. "Keep things civil or I'll toss you out of here on your—"

"Jasper!" Boone warned, cutting his grandfather off before he could get himself in trouble.

Paige bowed her head. She should have been used to being snubbed, but it still hurt to know she wasn't welcome in Love. If only they could understand she was acting only in the best interests of the town she loved so dearly. She was trying her best to be unselfish.

Cameron turned toward the townsfolk and glared at them. "Have some manners!" he growled. "Stop acting like a bunch of small-town bullies."

"Well said, grandson," Jasper said with an approving nod of his head. "Let's show some decorum. I'm now going to give Paige the floor. She has something of vital importance to discuss." Jasper wiggled his eyebrows. "And it has to do with this sizable check she brought made out to the town of Love." Jasper waved the check in the air.

Dwight turned up his nose as if he had smelled something foul. "This is highly irregular. You have no standing here, Paige Reynolds."

Paige met Dwight's beady eyes head-on. "I disagree. I happen to own property here in Love, which makes me a taxpayer and a resident."

"That's true," Declan shouted from the back of the room. "She has every right to come before us."

Dwight began to riffle through his bylaws. "I'm not sure one can just flit back into town after a two-year absence and try to conduct new business at a town meeting. Surely that's not allowed under the rules of order."

"There's no such stipulation," Hazel said in a crisp voice. "And this topic actually falls under old business, Dwight. It has to do with the cannery deal."

Dwight adjusted his spectacles. He pinched the bridge of his nose. "I believe that business concluded when Robert Reynolds stole from the town coffers and single-handedly put the kibosh on our plans." He tapped his chin. "Hmm…he then fled this jurisdiction, quickly followed, I might add, by his daughter. And now we're supposed to entertain a motion by said accomplice."

Cameron jumped to his feet. "What you just said is slanderous!" He began to make a motion as if he was going to approach the dais. "And if you breathe another word of that kind of talk, you and I are going to have a problem that might just require you to get a new pair of glasses."

Paige tugged at Cameron's arm and pulled him back to a seated position. "Cameron, don't waste your breath. The only thing Dwight understands is the bottom line. And in his mind I'm tainted by my father's guilt."

"He'd better watch the name-calling," Cameron seethed.

Paige looked over at Jasper. "Would you like to explain why I came back to Love or shall I?"

Jasper surprised her by grinning at her. "I think you've earned the right to tell this town the big news."

Dwight made an audible sound of outrage. His face resembled a thundercloud.

She looked to Cameron, who gave her a nod of encouragement. Paige stood up on trembling legs and turned toward the large audience. She cleared her throat and scanned the room for a friendly face. A few rows away a beautiful, dark-haired woman sent her an encouraging smile. It took only a moment for Paige to realize it was Grace, Boone's wife. She had seen her photo enough in media reports to recognize her stunning features.

Feeling slightly self-conscious, she fiddled with her

sleeves. "Good evening. Thank you, Mayor Prescott, for allowing me the floor. I'm Paige Reynolds. Most of you have known me for years. And you knew my father, Robert. Many of you were his friends." Her voice quivered a bit. "I know he let this town down. He let me down, too. I was raised by a man who taught me right from wrong. He guided me by solid principles. I don't know the exact reasons he went so far astray, but I do know that at the end of his life he deeply regretted his actions. He sought forgiveness. And redemption. With his last breath, he asked me to come back to Love. My father realized that the money he took wasn't enough to soothe the pain he caused by betraying this town. It's like the Bible says—'For what will it profit a man if he shall gain the whole world and lose his soul?'

"One of the reasons I came back was to return a portion of the funds he stole." Audible gasps could be heard among the townsfolk. "A very large sum that can help this town immensely. I want the money to do great things for Love. I know some of you might think that I have no right to have any say in this, but I'm committed to the financial growth of this town. That has never wavered. And I have the business background and education to support it."

"Thank you for the five-hankie moment," Dwight interrupted. "But what does all this have to do with anything? You've basically returned money that rightfully belonged to this town."

"Which she did of her own accord. No guilty person does that!" a voice shouted out from behind her. Paige turned around and caught sight of Honor, Cameron's younger sister. She was standing in the aisle, her long dark hair swirling, an irate expression stamped on her face. Paige wanted to sob at the sight of her. With her petite stature and delicate features, she didn't bear a resemblance to her brothers, but there was no question she was 100 percent Prescott.

"These interruptions are beyond the pale," Dwight said in a high-pitched voice that bordered on a screech. A few people openly snickered.

"This is a town meeting, Dwight. As residents of Love, we have a right to voice our thoughts and opinions," Grace said in an impassioned voice. "Otherwise it's a dictatorship."

"No young ladies want to move to a town in the wilds of Alaska that is known for being led by dictators," Myrtle shrieked. She was standing in the aisle next to Honor, dressed from head to toe in peacock print and rhinestones. Although mere days ago Paige had viewed her as a harridan, Myrtle was now beginning to grow on her.

Boone stood up and raised his fingers to his mouth. His loud whistle cut through the chaos. "Settle down, everyone," he said. A heavy silence ensued. It seemed no one wanted to mess with the town sheriff.

"I think we owe Paige an opportunity to finish what she was saying." Boone nodded in Paige's direction. "We're listening."

"I—I think this town should have a cannery. And it would have been up and running now if it hadn't been for my father. But the present situation doesn't have to stay that way. We…this town…can still move forward with the project. The influx of money can make it happen. It could pay for the completion of the building and all the start-up costs."

"And why should anyone trust you?" Dwight called out.

Paige refused to look at Dwight. She focused on the villagers. "Because I was raised here and I love it more than words can ever fully express. And I've brought my daughter here so she can grow to love it as much as her parents do. Emma is a Prescott and I want her to be proud of who she is. I want her to know that forgiveness and redemption are possible. And even though my father did something despicable, he taught me to tackle things head-on. That's what I'm trying to do. This town could grow financially by leaps and bounds if we're exporting canned fish products. And think of all the jobs there would be. With my business background, I think I could be an asset to the project." She swung her gaze around the audience. "Thank you for listening."

A smattering of loud applause broke out, accompanied by a few whistles. As Paige headed back to her seat, she realized that Cameron was clapping louder than anyone. Dwight was apoplectic. He was trying to say something, but the clapping drowned him out. She couldn't help but smile at her small victory. The room was pulsing with electricity. Although she knew not everyone in the room was cheering her on, it felt amazing that she actually had supporters. There were people here who believed in her and what she was hoping to accomplish.

Paige smoothed the back of her skirt and sat back down. Cameron reached over and squeezed her hand.

She blinked past the tears pricking her eyes and looked over at him. He winked at her. "Well done, Paige. Well done."

His supportive gesture was surprising since she knew he was still on the fence regarding her involvement in the stolen funds.

"Thank you for your discernment, Miss Reynolds. This matter will be taken up before the town council and will be voted upon by the villagers at a future meeting. I move that we conclude this meeting," Jasper said.

"I second it," Hazel said smoothly.

"Wait one minute," Dwight said in a raised voice just as Jasper banged his gavel down, effectively closing the meeting.

"Meeting adjourned," Jasper announced in a gleeful tone.

Before Paige could even gather her composure, she found herself surrounded by a group of residents. Old friends were grabbing her hand and patting her on the back, showering her with words of thanks and encouragement. Grace came up and gave her a hug. "It's so nice to meet you, Paige. It was so brave of you to come here tonight and address the town." Grace shuddered. "I've had to do it once or twice myself and can attest it isn't easy."

"I have to admit my knees were knocking," Paige said with a chuckle. "I'm surprised no one heard it."

Grace laughed along with her. "You've got spunk. I like that."

"Spoken by a woman who has plenty to go around," Boone said as he sidled up behind his wife and wrapped his arms around her waist. He placed a tender kiss on the side of her forehead that had Paige yearning for her own tall, dark and handsome Alaskan.

Hazel, Jasper and Myrtle joined her circle of supporters.

Myrtle stepped forward and reached for her hand. She patted it. "I appreciate your courage in coming back here, young lady. You have my full support. If there's anything you need moving forward, please don't hesitate to let me know." She sent Paige a knowing look. "As the local historian, I know this town like the back of my hand."

Paige smiled at Myrtle, feeling slightly overwhelmed by the crush of people. Most of them she knew, but there were a handful of young women who she suspected were in Alaska to find their other halves under Jasper's Operation Love program. They were smiling and upbeat and positive about her plan.

Without any fanfare, Honor stepped forward and stood before Paige, her sweet face wet with tears. "Oh, Paige, I've missed you so," Honor cried as she threw herself into Paige's arms.

"I've missed you, too, sweetie," Paige said as she hugged the young woman who had been like a sister to her. When everything had fallen apart for her in Love, Honor had been attending college out of state. They had never had a proper goodbye. Ashamed of her father's actions, Paige had never had the courage to reach out to Honor. Since Cameron had severed all ties with her, she hadn't felt right about dragging Honor into the whole mess.

When they pulled apart, Paige noticed Cameron standing nearby, his gaze trained on the two of them.

"Are you back for good?" Honor asked. There was such hope radiating from her eyes.

Back for good? It was a complicated question, one she didn't have a ready answer for. She didn't want to extinguish Honor's joy, but she couldn't give her false hope either. She had returned to Alaska for a specific purpose. Cameron was now aware of Emma's existence and he was beginning to form a bond with her. Fulfilling her father's dying wish was a bit trickier, but she was now one step closer to achieving it. If the town decided to proceed with the cannery project, Paige would relocate to Love for a period of time in order to support the project. She was hoping to be hired on to work as a consultant. At the moment everything was up in the air.

"To be honest, I'm not sure, honey," Paige said, reaching for Honor's hand and gripping it tightly. "If the cannery project doesn't pan out, it might make sense for us to return to Seattle. I don't know what the future holds, but I'm here now. And I can't wait for you to meet your niece."

Honor let out a little squeal and began to gush about Emma. She told Paige about completing graduate school and her plans to work in wildlife conservation in Alaska. They made plans to have lunch one afternoon and to catch up on everything they had missed in each other's lives.

Paige glanced in Cameron's direction just in time to see his retreating figure as he quietly slipped out of the room. She felt a hitch in the region of her heart upon seeing him walk away from her. He was the only one with whom she really wanted to celebrate this moment. Although she appreciated every last gesture of support, Cameron's presence was the one she craved. More and more she found herself relying on him like a lifeline the same way she had done in the past. Although her head knew he no longer belonged to her, it seemed her heart still hadn't got the message.

It was still light outside when Cameron left the town hall building and headed back toward the Moose Café. His truck was parked out in the lot behind his establishment. As he walked along Jarvis Street, he paused to peer in shop windows. In many ways this downtown area was the heart and pulse of Love. Despite the financial slump, the wheels were still turning for the shop owners and proprietors. Not a single shop had closed its doors. The town had rallied from within and supported all the businesses so that no one went under. It had been extraordinary. No matter what problems Love faced, his hometown was remarkable.

He was wrangling with feelings way too complicated for him to even process at the moment. Paige had made him so proud tonight by speaking out on behalf of the cannery. She had been brave and honorable and very ambitious. He had almost stopped breathing when Honor had asked Paige about her long-term plans. After flying high on the heels of Paige's rousing speech, his spirits had plummeted once he realized that Paige and Emma in all likelihood would not remain in Love. Suddenly the threat of them leaving hung over him like a dark cloud.

His life was better with them in it. Emma was a Prescott and he wanted her to live here in Alaska and be right in the thick of his big, spirited family. Maybe he was being selfish, but he wanted to be her father in every sense of the word. He still hadn't spent much quality time with her, just snatches here and there. He wanted his daughter to play with his nephew, Aidan, and learn how to skate at Deer Run Lake. The thought of not seeing her on Christmas morning gutted him. It would be such a blessing to watch her rip open presents and sit next to her in the pew at church.

He was so tired of losing people in his life. His mother. His father. Ruby. Paige. He had already lost precious time with his daughter. It would be agonizing to say goodbye to his child. His mind was whirling with the details of the conversation he had overheard between Paige and Honor.

I don't know what the future holds.

Before he knew it, he had reached the back lot. He stepped up into his truck and revved the engine, hoping to drown out his thoughts. Paige's words burned in his ears. Had she come back only to leave again?

How could she even consider separating him from his daughter? Hadn't she already done that for fourteen long months? Anger rose up inside him. He slammed his fist on the steering wheel. Resentment began to consume him. Knowing this wasn't the way, Cameron lowered his head onto the steering wheel. It was this type of quick-burning fury that had got him into this situation in the first place. Two years ago he had chosen to believe the worst of Paige when he hadn't had all the facts at his disposal. Now that she had made him aware of her trust fund, all of her actions made sense. For the first time he was forcing himself to look in the mirror and accept the role he had played in Paige leaving Love.

Lord, please help me. I don't want this rage to consume me any longer. I'm so tired of feeling helpless against the things in my life that cause me strife and anxiety. I am trying to be a better man, one who is more focused on what's ahead of me than what's behind me. I want Emma to be proud to call me Daddy.

He began to take calming breaths. Within seconds the anger dissipated. "Thank You, Lord," he whispered. Rage didn't have any place in his world now. From this point forward his existence was all about a pint-size cutie who had wormed her way into his heart in record time. He needed to be the best man possible for her. A man driven by faith and not fear. And because of the all-consuming love he felt for Emma, he was going to do everything in his power to make sure that she stayed right here in Love where she belonged.

Chapter Eight

Even after Sophie's return to work after her illness, Cameron still continued to ask Paige to fill in a few hours here and there at the Moose Café. Paige loved working at the café. Perhaps it was the customers. Most were kind and regaled her with funny stories about Love or bits of town gossip. Of course, every now and again she would run up against a customer who wanted to rant and rave about her father. She had learned to deal with those situations with grace and an open heart. If God wanted to use her as a vessel for forgiveness, she was willing to be His instrument. She loved the hustle and bustle of the place and the smell of coffee floating in the air. And she loved the fact that Cameron knew he could rely on her. It made her feel wanted and needed. It was her fervent hope that one of these days he would come to his senses and realize that she hadn't been in collusion with her father. At least that way Emma would never pick up on any strained vibes between her parents.

Most days when she filled in, Fiona drove in with her

so that Cameron could spend a little time with Emma. Cameron seemed to love those moments. Paige knew she had done the right thing in returning to Love when she watched the playful interaction between father and daughter. Somehow it eased the grieving process she was going through for her own father. Day by day the ache of loss was beginning to lessen.

During her afternoon break Cameron approached her as she was digging in to a grilled turkey-and-avocado sandwich with a side of kale chips. He'd made her one of his new creations. A white-chocolate mochaccino. Although one sip of it confirmed it was rich and calorie laden, she wasn't going to fret about it. She was feeling self-indulgent today.

"Hey, Paige. I have an Emma question. Is it my imagination or am I growing on her?" Cameron asked.

Paige swallowed a bite of her sandwich. She tried not to groan out loud at how good it was. "It's not your imagination. She lights up when she sees you. And she's very comfortable in your presence."

"I thought so!" Cameron said, his voice full of excitement. "She doesn't give me that 'Who's he?' look anymore."

Paige laughed at the visual. Emma had a very expressive face and she knew that particular look very well. She had always called it Emma's grandpa face since she tended to scrunch up her nose like a little old man. "Believe me, that's progress. When Fiona first came to us, it took Emma a long time to accept her. Now she adores her."

"So, do you think I can spend some alone time with

her this weekend?" Cameron tossed the question out casually but she could see the expectant expression etched on his face.

Although she had logically known this day would come, she didn't feel prepared. Not by a long shot. She put her sandwich back down on her plate. "Do you think you're ready for that?" Paige asked. She was biting her lip. Suddenly her pulse was beating erratically at the idea of Emma being taken from her normal setting.

"I take it you don't." Immediately he sounded defensive.

"No, it's not that. It's just that Emma gets fussy sometimes and she's really hard to get down for her nap. And she's pretty finicky about meals." She found herself rattling off a litany of reasons. "She's also been having these issues with allergies. Some foods like strawberries and peas have been giving her an allergic reaction."

Cameron crossed his arms. He frowned down at Paige. "Something tells me you could come up with a hundred reasons why I can't spend some one-on-one time with my daughter."

For a moment she felt like a deer caught in the headlights. Cameron's eyes were like laser beams boring a hole straight through her. She opened her mouth, then snapped it shut.

"You're right. I'm sorry," she apologized. "This is all new for me. It's only ever been me. And Fiona. And lots of support from God along the way. Emma had a great bond with my dad but he was too ill to take care of her." She shrugged. "I suppose I'm having a little trouble letting go."

"She's safe with me. I'd never let any harm come to her. Not on my watch." His expression was so fierce it almost made Paige laugh. But she knew he was serious. He was fighting for some quality time with Emma and she had no right to stand between them. After all, she had come back to Alaska for this very reason. So Cameron could forge a bond with Emma. There was no point in putting roadblocks in his path.

"I know, Cameron. It isn't that I don't think she's safe with you. I just need someone to cut the cord I've had tethered to me since the day she was born." Paige's voice cracked with emotion.

He placed a hand on her shoulder. "Hey. Nobody's asking you to cut off any ties. I just need to establish something between Emma and myself that is separate and apart from you. It's wonderful that you've acted as a bridge between us, but at some point I have to step up as a strong presence in her life."

"I get it. And I have to admit that in the beginning I was really worried about the lure of the Prescott family. I kept thinking that you had so much to offer Emma. It's hard sometimes to deal with the fact that she has no family on my side other than myself. There are no bells and whistles. No little cousins to run around with or a treasure-hunting grandpa to hang out with."

"She has you. That in itself is amazing. And Jasper hung up his treasure-hunting days when Grace discovered that the Prescott ancestors didn't strike it rich in gold. No more spelunking for him!"

"Oh no. What a shame," Paige said. "He must have

been devastated after believing in that Prescott family legend for so long."

Cameron shrugged. "Sometimes when one dream dies, it's time to find another one. How does Saturday sound for Emma? I've taken the day off."

"That will be fine," she agreed with a nod, wishing she still didn't have qualms about Emma spending the day with Cameron without her.

As he walked away to take care of a customer, Paige couldn't get Cameron's comment out of her mind. Giving up on a dream wasn't half as easy as he believed. She had once imagined a life with him—until those visions had crumbled into dust. Even though she had stopped fantasizing about a future with Cameron years ago, all of a sudden she couldn't stop thinking about what might have been if events hadn't altered the course of their relationship.

Marriage? A cozy house with a view of the mountains?

She immediately chided herself for taking this sentimental trip down memory lane. Aspirations were wonderful things, but it wasn't wise to continue to fantasize about things that would never come to pass.

Cameron wiped his brow as he quietly shut the door on the guest room he had transformed into a makeshift nursery. It still had a long way to go before it was sugar, spice and pink teddy bears, but he was committed to finishing the room with a fresh coat of paint and all the trimmings.

After running him ragged for the past few hours,

Emma had finally settled down for a nap. But not before calling out for her mama numerous times. Finally, out of sheer exhaustion she had drifted off into slumber on his shoulder. Using an equal measure of agility and finesse, he had placed her down in the crib that had been passed on to him by Liam. At first he had felt guilty about taking the crib that Liam had built with his own hands for Aidan, but his brother had insisted. Something about it had felt wrong, as if Liam didn't believe he would ever find love again and add to his family.

Why hadn't anyone told him how difficult it was to watch a fourteen-month-old for a few hours? The diaper change had thrown him for a loop. He scratched his head, still feeling unsure as to whether he had put the thing on correctly. And she had been fidgeting so much that he'd ripped a few of them while trying to change her.

Did the diapers even fit properly? Her pudgy little legs had looked crammed in. He didn't want her legs to chafe against it, thus giving Paige evidence of his deficiencies in the baby-watching department.

He let out a grunt. Was he really standing here worrying about diapers? It was amazing how much self-doubt could arise when child care was involved.

Cameron was pretty sure he had sprinkled her with so much baby powder that she resembled a powdered doughnut. But it wasn't as if Paige had given him a how-to manual. Sure, she had passed on a few tips, but he was flying by the seat of his pants.

Out of sheer desperation he had placed an SOS call to Liam, telling him he needed his assistance immediately. Liam had promised to come over as soon as possible. Cameron hadn't mentioned anything to his brother during the phone call about watching Emma for the day.

Within fifteen minutes he heard the screech of tires in his driveway. Before Liam could even let himself in, Cameron jerked the door open to greet him. With his dark hair and rangy build, he bore a passing resemblance to him and Boone. Girls had always claimed Liam had a soulful and sensitive vibe. Like Honor, he was tenderhearted.

"I don't think I've ever been so happy to see somebody in my life." Cameron felt his whole body sag with relief.

"What's the emergency?" Liam asked as he stepped inside the house. He was looking all around with a frantic expression. "You said it wasn't anything medical, but it sounded urgent."

"It's Emma." He put his fingers up to his lips. "Shh. I just put her down for her nap."

"You didn't mention she was here." Liam frowned. "Did something happen?" he whispered.

"I've been watching her for the last four hours. You know how it is. Parent-child bonding time. But I think I may be in way over my head. She's been a little... Um, how should I put this? Challenging?"

Liam's jaw dropped. He stood as still as a statue. "That's the urgent matter you called me over here for? You have got to be kidding me."

Cameron frowned. "Hey! Have a little compassion."

Liam folded his arms across his chest and shook his head. "Here's my advice. Man up, little brother."

"I am manning up. I just needed some backup just in case." His voice trailed off. He wasn't sure how to put his concerns into words.

Liam scoffed. "In case what? She's a little over a year old. Are you afraid she's going to explode or something? Get a grip!"

Cameron gulped. "I've been reading this book. It's called *How to Tame a Toddler* and it's a runaway bestseller. Problem is, none of that stuff worked with Emma."

Liam raised an eyebrow. "Tame? She's not a circus animal."

Cameron rolled his eyes. "It's just that I need some pointers from someone who's been there. She was crying for quite a bit," he admitted, wincing at the memory of Emma's heartbreaking wails. "I almost caved in and called Paige."

"If she cries, try to see what's wrong. Check her diaper. See if she's thirsty or hungry," Liam suggested.

"Gee, why didn't I think of that?" Cameron drawled.

Liam gritted his teeth. "'Bye, Cameron," he said in a clipped tone.

"No! Sorry. It just slipped out. I'm a little bit fried at the moment. Please don't go." Cameron pulled at his brother's arm.

Liam turned back toward him. "What are you so panicky about, anyway? She's a baby."

"A baby I'm just getting to know." Cameron raked his hand through his hair and let out a ragged sigh. "I'm not feeling sorry for myself, but I missed out on the first months of caring for Emma. I should be a pro at this by now, but instead I'm floundering."

Liam touched Cameron on the shoulder. "That was a tough break, you missing out on all that time with her. I can't imagine not having experienced Aidan's first moments. I know this hasn't been easy for you. And believe it or not, all first-time fathers have fears and doubts. It's perfectly normal."

A feeling of sadness enveloped him. "I'm trying not to wallow in it. And I know I'm blessed to have Emma, but I hate this feeling that I'm never going to be able to make up for lost time."

"You can't turn back the clock, Cam. But what you can do is be there one hundred percent for your daughter from this point forward. You can get to know her day by day, moment by moment. Children are resilient. And as long as you nurture them, love them and keep 'em safe and protected, you can consider yourself a very accomplished father."

Cameron let go of the deep breath he had been holding. "I think that I can do all of those things. Especially the love part." He grinned at his brother as excitement rose up inside him. Fatherhood was going to be a journey, one he was looking forward to tremendously. He was already anticipating moments such as bringing her to her first day of nursery school and taking her sledding at Deer Run Lake. And like Liam had said, every father harbored fears. It was how he tackled those fears that would determine his future with Emma.

"You're going to be an excellent father, Cam. You're well on your way," Liam said.

Hearing those words from his big brother meant the world to him. Liam was an amazing dad, one who had raised Aidan in the shadow of a tragedy that had threatened to pull Liam under. Because of Aidan, his brother had fought his way through that dark time and emerged a stronger father than ever to his little boy. If Cameron could be half the father Liam was, he'd consider himself a success.

All of a sudden he heard soft cries from the baby monitor.

"That was a quick nap," he grumbled. "Let me go check in on her. Maybe I can get her back to sleep."

"Or not," Liam said with a smirk. Cameron scowled at his brother. He was pretty sure Liam was enjoying seeing him a little bit frazzled. He walked a few feet down the hall until he reached the nursery. Cameron wrinkled up his nose as soon as he opened the door.

"What's going on?" Liam asked from right behind him.

He turned toward his brother. "There's a baby in there who doesn't smell too good."

Liam threw back his head and chuckled. "Dirty-diaper duty. It's part of the terrain, Cam."

"Hey, you wouldn't want to show me how it's done, would you? Show me the ropes?" he asked hopefully.

"Listen, this is a rite of passage. It's a dad thing. You've got to do this and take it on the chin." He gave him a thumbs-up sign. "No worries. You've got this."

"Thanks, Liam," he muttered as he entered the room and advanced toward Emma's crib. She was lying on her back and looking up at the mobile he had just placed on the ceiling yesterday. It was a sun, moon and stars. At night they lit up with a phosphorescent glow. Despite her earlier cries, she now seemed content to babble and stare up at the whirling figures.

Cameron gazed down at her, overwhelmed by the depth of his love for this sweet, amazing child. He wouldn't trade her for anything, dirty diapers and all. Just then Emma looked up at him and gifted him with a beatific smile. She began to pump her little legs in the air and reached her hands up toward him.

"Dada. Dada," Emma cried out. "Up. Me up."

It felt as if all the air had just left his lungs in one single breath. Dada! For a single moment everything went still and he had to lean against the crib railing for support. His knees threatened to give out underneath him.

Cameron reached down and lifted her into his arms. He cradled her against his chest as he fought back tears. *Dada.* She had said the most precious word in the universe. He felt like throwing his fist up in the air in triumph, but he didn't want to startle Emma. No, he would act as cool as a cucumber even though he wanted to jump up and down.

This moment would be forever imprinted on him like a tattoo. Someday he would describe this event to Emma in excruciating detail. He might even tell her about her dirty diaper just to see her roll her eyes at him. For now, he simply wanted to savor this blessing.

God was good. A few weeks ago he hadn't even been aware of his daughter's existence. And now she was firmly embedded in his heart. He had officially fallen in love with his baby girl.

* * *

Paige checked her watch again as she waited in her car at the end of Cameron's driveway. After counting down the minutes until she could be reunited with Emma, she'd decided to just wait near his home. She'd arrived about forty-five minutes ago, but thankfully, her car was hidden from view by a copse of spruce trees. She didn't want Cameron to think she didn't trust him with their daughter. It wasn't about him. It was about her attachment to Emma and her having to adjust to the idea of co-parenting. For so long her daughter's care had rested on her shoulders as the sole custodial parent.

This too shall pass. Once they got into a routine, she would be fine. She wouldn't be lurking in her car with a pang in her soul.

Finally, at exactly four o'clock on the dot she was standing at Cameron's front stoop pressing the doorbell.

When he opened the door, she let out an involuntary sigh. Emma was resting at his hip and he looked like an impossibly handsome, rugged father—the type who would be featured on the cover of a trendy magazine. *Alaskan Dad.* Laughter bubbled up inside her at the thought of it.

"How was everything?" Paige asked, resisting the urge to scoop Emma up in her arms. It was reassuring to see her daughter so secure with Cameron. Every little girl needed a daddy to adore her.

"She's still in one piece," Cameron teased. "And so am I."

Paige laughed as Cameron ushered her inside his house. Emma, like most babies her age, could be a handful. Something about Cameron's expression told her that she had indeed pushed him to the limit. "She pretty much blew me away by calling me Dada," Cameron said in a voice bursting with pride. "Not just once, mind you. Several times."

She turned toward him and grinned, knowing how much he had wanted this moment. "I'm so happy for you. That type of moment is priceless."

They'd made their way to Cameron's living room and she saw Liam standing there smiling warmly at her. He held his arms open to her and she walked straight into a bear hug. Of all three of the Prescott boys, Liam was the most demonstrative one.

"I can't believe we're seeing each other again after all these years and under these circumstances." Liam looked over at Emma. "Your daughter is one beautiful little girl. Thankfully, she looks like you and not her father. She dodged a bullet," Liam teased.

"Ha-ha. Very funny," Cameron said.

"So far everyone else seems to think she looks just like her dad, so I'm hoping to see some of myself in her personality," Paige said.

"I think I might have caught a little bit of that similarity today," Cameron drawled, the corners of his mouth twitching with merriment.

Liam covered his grin with his hand and jabbed Cameron in the side. Paige didn't know what the inside joke was but she raised an eyebrow at Cameron.

"Aidan keeps asking about his little baby cousin, so we'll have to arrange a meeting really soon," Liam said.

"That would be great to get the kids together," Paige said.

"Will you be at the spring festival tomorrow?" Liam asked.

"I didn't realize it was tomorrow, but I think Emma would like it." She shot a glance at Cameron, who nodded enthusiastically.

Paige reached for Liam's hand and clasped it tightly. "I was so sorry to hear about Ruby. She was one of the most amazing human beings I've ever known." Exotic, down-to-earth Ruby. She had been the perfect counterpart to Liam. Together they'd made a beautiful couple.

A look of sadness flickered across his face. "She thought the world of you. I'm very thankful she had a friend like you, Paige. And please accept my condolences about your father. I know that losing him must have shaken you to your core. The two of you were very close."

Just then Cameron put Emma down on the carpet. Liam's eyes trailed after her and he got down on his haunches to play with her.

Tears gathered in Paige's eyes at the magnitude of Liam's loss. His poor son would never know firsthand the amazing woman who had brought him into this world. Overcome with emotion, she quietly slipped out of the room and through the sliding glass door in the kitchen that led to the outside deck. Once she was outside, she trained her attention on the mountains looming in the distance and the clean, fresh air she was deeply inhaling.

A sound alerted her to Cameron's presence behind her. She knew it was him before he uttered a word.

"Hey, what is it? What's wrong?" he asked, swiftly reaching her side.

She swiped at the tears with the back of her hand. "It's nothing. I'm just being a sentimental fool."

"It's not nothing. You're crying," he said as he studied her.

She nodded. What was the use in denying it? The evidence was all over her face.

"Since I've been back, not a single person has offered me condolences for my father's death. Not a single one. Until now. Until Liam spoke the words no one else could manage to pass through their lips. And talking about Ruby and then hearing Liam say he was sorry about my father's passing… It was just too much all at once." She shivered as a cool breeze swept over her, then wrapped her arms around her middle.

He reached for her hand and entwined it with his own. "I'm sorry I never extended my condolences to you about your father. I'm ashamed of that." Cameron sucked his teeth. "I've been so angry at Robert. He was my friend and mentor and the smartest man I've ever known. Because my own father has been absent so much, he became a surrogate father to me. He didn't just betray this town. He betrayed me personally. It felt like I had been stabbed in the back. They say never to put mere mortals on pedestals, but I think I put your father on one, so when it all came crashing down, it was devastating."

He winced. "But my resentment toward him is separate and apart from the loss of him and what he meant to you. And what he used to mean to me."

"I know, Cam. I was angry with him, too. Because of his actions, I lost everything that mattered to me the most. Our relationship. This town and everyone in it. My saving grace was our daughter. It's hard to live in bitterness when you wake up every morning to a smiling baby who relies on you for everything. Feeling resentment toward him would only have weighed me down. And because of Emma, I couldn't afford that. The price would have been way too high."

"I guess I've been paying that fee for two years," Cameron said. "All this time I've been struggling to work through those feelings. I guess I haven't done a very good job of it." His jaw tensed.

"I know he hurt you. And believe it or not, he was very sorry about letting you down." She looked into Cameron's eyes. They appeared to be a vivid green at the moment and they shimmered with emotion. "He gave me a letter to give to you. I don't blame you if you want to rip it up and throw it in the trash, but I promised him I would hand it over to you."

Cameron knit his dark brows together. "A letter? For me? What does it say?" Suddenly his features tensed up.

"The letter is sealed, not to mention it wasn't meant for me to open. It was for your eyes only. I never would have betrayed that trust. I put the letter in the dining room hutch at the homestead. It's right by the little crystal owl. It's yours to take."

"I'm stunned that he wrote to me," Cameron said. His eyes were wide. And full of anxiety.

"Cameron. He loved you like a son. On some level I think you know that," Paige said.

Cameron laughed hollowly. "I'm not sure that I understand that kind of love. He left me holding the bag. For all he knew, I could have been prosecuted for the missing funds."

He was voicing all the things she had struggled with for so long until she had let it all go in an effort to heal her wounded heart.

"Love is imperfect. And I think he left enough of a trail so that it was clear he was the culprit. I think on some level he was trying to make it known that he was responsible." Paige knew from having spoken to her father at length that he had deliberately left breadcrumbs in his wake so that she and Cameron wouldn't be considered as accomplices. Sadly, both of them had still been cast under suspicion.

"It still doesn't explain why. Why would he wound so many people?" Cameron looked utterly bewildered.

"Hurt people hurt people. Ruby used to say that expression all the time. I never fully understood it until recently. He was in a lot of emotional pain for years and desperate to get out of a financial hole he dug for himself."

"Emotional pain? Because of your mother?" Cameron asked. "I know he struggled for a long time after her death."

"That's part of it. He was driving the car that day when my mother was killed. I don't think he ever dealt with his guilt about being the driver. He walked away without a scratch, but his whole world came crashing down around him when she died as a result of her injuries." She held up her hands. "Again, I'm not defending him. I'm just trying to provide some sort of reference point for his colossal betrayal."

"How in the world did you manage to forgive him?" The tone of Cameron's voice was incredulous.

"It wasn't easy. But having Emma brought everything into sharp focus. Forgiveness isn't just a gift for the one who's forgiven. It's a blessing for me, as well. I couldn't carry all of his sins on my shoulders, and I surely didn't want to harbor hatred in my heart."

Cameron heaved a tremendous sigh. "I thought I had stopped harboring bad feelings against my parents for walking away from us, but I haven't been able to let it go. Not fully."

"If you do, you'll lighten your own burdens. It won't just benefit you. Think of Emma and what it will mean for her. Both your parents are still living. You still have time to reach out to them and forge a new beginning." Her voice went soft. "At least you have that option."

Cameron nodded. "I'm sorry you don't have that choice, but thanks for reminding me that I still do."

He leaned in and placed his arm around her. She laid her head on his shoulder and enjoyed the quiet splendor of the Alaskan afternoon. Everything was still and quiet, and there wasn't a cloud in the sky. An eagle dipped down long enough that they could admire it before soaring back up toward the mountain and its nest. She closed her eyes and imagined that Cameron had not a single doubt about her. For just one carefree moment she could pretend that they were still in love and that nothing had ever torn them apart.

Chapter Nine

The next morning dawned bright and beautiful. A radiant sun shimmered from above. The sky was a clear cornflower blue. The temperature was practically balmy. It was a perfect day for the spring festival. The event, held every year on May 1, was a town tradition in Love. It was a widely attended community gathering with a variety of activities—a pie bake-off, kiddie rides, a battle of the bands, a quilting competition, arts and crafts, athletic contests and more. There was also a blessing-of-the-fleet ceremony down by the pier. Since fishermen had always been important to the Love economy, it was a way of honoring them and their boats.

For as long as Cameron could remember, he had attended the festival. As a kid, he had always looked forward to the whipped-cream-eating contest. He chuckled at the memory of all the first-place ribbons he had won, much to his mother's chagrin. Mama. He hadn't thought of her in a while. If he was being honest with himself, he had made little or no effort to keep in contact with her over the past few years. Maybe that needed to change. He owed it to Emma to at least try.

He had decided to close the doors of the café at 11:00 a.m. this morning. There was no way in the world he was going to miss Emma's first festival. And most of the town would be too busy enjoying the activities to stop in at the Moose Café. He had driven to the festivities with Hazel, who was eager to attend her first festival since being coupled up with Jasper. Cameron had been skeptical when they'd first started dating. Both of them were opinionated and forceful. He hadn't been of the belief that they'd last a week. Over the past few months they had grown on him as a couple. Hazel brought out Jasper's sweet side, while Jasper elicited a tenderness in Hazel he hadn't seen before. It was shaping up to be a great partnership.

Once they had arrived, Cameron found himself scouring the fairgrounds for Paige and Emma.

"You look like you're going to jump out of your skin," Hazel noted as she looked up at him.

"I'm excited to spend time with my girl," Cameron said, rubbing his hands together. "Paige said she would bring her around eleven thirty."

"Which girl are you talking about?" Hazel asked with a sly grin.

Cameron sent her a quizzical look. "There's only one girl in my life. And that's Emma. She's all that I need."

Hazel snorted. "She's a baby, Cameron. It's great that you two are bonding, but still need romance."

He held up his hands. "Things didn't go so well the

last go-round. Not sure I'm ready to throw my hat in the ring again."

What he did know was that he didn't want his heart handed to him on a platter again.

"If you think I don't see the way you light up when Paige is around, you must think I'm a blind fool."

Cameron groaned. "We have history. Not to mention we have a child. Plus, she's a gorgeous woman. Who wouldn't light up around her?"

Hazel put her hands on her hips. "So what are you going to do about it?"

"Nothing! She might not be staying in Love, Hazel. If this cannery thing doesn't pan out, she might head back to Seattle."

The older woman let out a groan. "Oh no, Cam. Would she really go back to Seattle? After making such an effort to come back here and right Robert's wrongs? Not to mention you and Emma are getting on like a house on fire. I can't even imagine!"

He clenched his teeth. "That's not the only issue standing between us. I still don't know if I can trust her."

Hazel's eyes resembled storm clouds. "Cameron Prescott! I was one of the most vocal people in town who spoke out against Paige. I'm ashamed of that now. She's a good woman, Cam. She's shown it over and over again ever since she stepped foot back in this town. It's time for you to man up and take a good look at why you're so intent on believing the worst about her. Why can't you see what's staring you straight in the face?

And I'll be offering up prayers on your behalf that you come to your senses before she leaves town."

He shrugged, stuffing down the emotions that threatened to swallow him up whole. The thought of losing Paige all over again terrified him. But how could he lay his emotions on the line when he had no idea if his heart was going to be ripped out of his chest again? And this time it would be far worse, because if Paige left Alaska, she would be taking his daughter with her. The very idea of so much loss made him shut down a little.

"It's pretty obvious you're guarding your heart, Cameron." Hazel stared at him with a knowing look.

"Let's just say I'm playing it safe," Cameron said. "I have no idea how she feels about me."

"Don't you? Then you're not half as smart as I thought you were." Hazel began making a tutting sound. "No good comes from keeping your emotions under lock and key. Take a page from Boone's handbook. He laid it all on the line. He threw fear out the window to chase Gracie down and profess his love to her. And if I remember correctly, you cheered him on."

"That was a little different," Cameron grumbled. "They didn't share a tortured history. There wasn't so much baggage between them."

Hazel jabbed him in the side, causing him to let out a howl of pain.

Cameron rubbed his side. "Hey! What was that for? You've been spending too much time with Jasper. He's been rubbing off on you."

She snapped her fingers in front of his face. "Wake

up! You're wasting time. If you still think Paige is the one who sets your heart afire, then get after it already."

"Shh, Hazel. Here come Paige and Emma," Cameron said as he spotted them about ten feet away. Paige was pushing the little girl in a bright green stroller. Emma was waving to everyone they passed by. Paige looked casual yet elegant in a pair of skinny jeans and a light blue cardigan sweater.

"Good morning," she called out as she approached them. Emma began waving wildly, which caused them to chuckle. "What a beautiful day for a festival."

"God sure did grant us favor today with this weather," Hazel said.

"Hey there, little miss," Cameron said, reaching out and tickling her under her chin.

"Dada!" Emma cooed, and Cameron almost passed out with joy. He couldn't imagine hearing Emma call him Dada ever getting old. It was a wondrous thing to be her father.

"Such a smart little girl," Jasper commented as he walked up. "This next generation of Prescotts are going to be something else."

"I won't argue with you about that," Cameron said, tickled by Jasper's acknowledgment of Emma. Even though he butted heads quite frequently with his grandfather, he respected and admired him more than he could ever express in words.

"Look who's here," Hazel said in a raised voice.

Liam and Aidan came into view as they headed in their direction. Aidan was running ahead of his father, his face lit up with exuberance.

"Hey! Dad says I can try to win a fish to take home," his nephew exclaimed in an excited voice. "Maybe I can try to win three or four of 'em."

"I think we have a one-fish limit at our house," Liam added with a bemused shake of his head.

Cameron reached over and ruffled Aidan's curly brown hair, realizing for the first time that he and Emma shared the same coloring.

The little boy gifted him with a sweet smile. Cameron raised his hand and Aidan slapped it enthusiastically. "High five, Uncle Cam," he said with a giggle.

"Ouch," Cameron said, pretending that he'd been hit hard. His nephew covered his mouth and laughed even harder.

"Daddy said you have a baby." Aidan looked over and pointed at Emma. "Is that her?"

"Yep, buddy. That's her. Her name is Emma and she's your cousin."

Aidan wrinkled his nose. "She's so little. Can I still play with her?"

"She's little, but before you know it, she won't be so small anymore," Cameron explained. He lowered his voice. "Don't tell anybody, but with the way she's been eating, I think she might grow into a giant."

The sound of Aidan's tinkling laughter rang out in the quiet afternoon. "No way," Aidan said with a shake of his head. "She's going to be a lady, not a giant."

Cameron threw back his head and laughed. Everyone else chuckled along with him.

"I'm Emma's mom, Aidan. I knew you a long time ago, but you probably don't remember."

Paige stepped forward and stuck out her hand, bending over at the waist. "And this little lady is Emma."

Aidan glanced at Emma, then reached out and grabbed her fingers. The little girl looked thoroughly delighted. She tugged on Aidan's fingers and let loose with a burst of giggles.

"Why don't we walk around and see what's going on," Liam suggested. "A little birdie told me that a certain town sheriff is sitting at the pie booth."

Cameron stopped in his tracks. He looked over at Liam. "Seriously? We can pay to throw a pie in his face?"

"Rumor has it," Liam said with a chuckle. "Wonder what the going rate is."

"Does it matter?" Cameron joked. "We're in, regardless."

"Can I throw a pie?" Aidan asked, jumping up and down with excitement.

"Of course you can," Cameron said. He dug into his pants pocket and pulled out some bills. "Matter of fact, the first one is on me." Aidan took the money and took off like a flash. Liam increased his stride so that he wasn't far behind him.

As they began walking as a group toward the booth, Cameron reached for Emma's stroller handle. "I'll take a turn, if you don't mind," he offered.

"Of course," Paige said as she let go of the handle. "It's nice to let someone take over for a change."

Cameron felt a burst of happiness explode in his chest. Being surrounded by his family members and Paige on this perfect spring day was making him believe in things he had thought were near impossible. He was learning moment by moment that life was really full of the most unexpected surprises.

Watching Boone get creamed in the face with pies was way more entertaining than Paige would ever admit. The Prescott brothers were practically giddy at the opportunity to smash the dessert in their brother's mug. Boone took it in stride, letting it be known to one and all that he was willing to do it for a good cause, Honor's wildlife organization. Finally, after several turns in line, Grace made Liam and Cameron move along and find another event at the festival to participate in. Although Grace was a sweetheart, it was apparent that no one wanted to mess with her protective side. It was sweet, Paige thought, how she stayed nearby with a towel so she could clean her husband up between pie throws. She watched as Boone placed a tender kiss on his wife's lips.

It was a simple yet romantic gesture that spoke volumes about their love. She let out a sigh. Once upon a time she and Cameron had felt that way about each other. They had been inseparable, finishing each other's sentences, fueling each other's dreams and bolstering one another when things in their lives became rocky.

Those old feelings for Cameron were returning and becoming stronger each and every day. She was falling back in love with him, even though she knew that it was risky. The events of two years ago had shown her in the most brutal way that caring for someone was a pathway to heartache. Yes, she believed in love in all its imperfections. But she didn't know if she could trust Cameron long enough to see if they had a shot at a future together. He had proved to her that the feelings he had felt for her weren't strong enough to withstand the whispers and smears of the townsfolk. His disloyalty had blindsided her. And Emma didn't need to get caught in the cross fire again. It would be confusing and upsetting for a little girl to see her parents at odds.

Not that Cameron had indicated in any way, shape or form that he was interested in pursuing a relationship with her. But they had got close again. And every now and then there was something hovering in between them that had nothing to do with friendship. It was as if all the air left the room when they were together. Sometimes it felt as if she couldn't breathe normally in his presence.

She heaved a deep sigh. How had this happened? How had her feelings for Cameron shifted so quickly?

After a while everyone splintered off into groups. Hazel was attached at the hip to Emma. Paige thought it was very heartwarming how her little girl seemed to enjoy being held in the other woman's arms. And Hazel lit up like sunshine when Emma was around. Perhaps, Paige thought, Emma would have a grandma in Love after all.

As everyone made their way off to different events, Paige found herself alone with Cameron. Hazel and Jasper had taken the kids to the livestock enclosure while Liam went off in search of Honor. Grace had been feeling dehydrated, so Boone took her to sit in the shade with an ice-cold water.

Suddenly, with the two of them being on their own, it reminded her of all the festivals they had attended together over the years. It brought back a tide of memories that swept over her like a gentle breeze. One of her first youthful dates with Cameron had taken place at this very fair. At seventeen years old, he had been a bit brash, and he'd gone to extreme lengths to win her more stuffed animals than she could hold in her arms. He'd walked around with a bit of swagger and she hadn't quite known what to make of him. By the end of the festival, he had revealed his tender side by telling her about his parents' divorce and how he was overprotective of his little sister. In that very moment Paige had known that Cameron Prescott would be tied to her forever.

And she had been right. Now they would always be inextricably linked together because of Emma.

"You know what I could go for?" Cameron asked, drawing her out of her trip down memory lane.

"Is it round and gooey and comes on a stick?" she asked in a playful voice, knowing full well that Cameron was referencing his love of caramel apples.

He rubbed his stomach. "I've been thinking about caramel apples for days."

"Well, lead the way," Paige said with a laugh. "I don't want to deprive you of your delicacy."

Cameron grabbed her by the hand and led her to the area of the festival where the food vendors were located. He gave a triumphant cry as he spotted the truck where the caramel apples were being sold.

"Do you want one?" he asked as he stood in line.

"No, thanks," Paige said. "I'm holding out for some iced lemonade."

"Suit yourself."

Once it was in his hands, he took a huge bite and groaned loudly with appreciation. As Paige stood there watching him with amusement, he continued to devour his treat.

"If I remember correctly, you used to love these, too. Sure you don't want the last bite?" he asked, holding up the final sliver.

She took a gentle bite, ending up with a trail of caramel dribbling down her chin. With a flick of his wrist, he tossed the stick in a nearby garbage can, then reached out and wiped the caramel away with the tip of his finger. Their eyes met and held. Something simmered and crackled between them. A deep and heavy vibe pulsed in the air.

Cameron dipped his head down and placed his lips on Paige's. He moved them over hers with sweetness, reaching out to cradle the sides of her face with his hands. This tender, soul-stirring kiss almost caused her knees to buckle. This moment had been years in the making. In the lonely moments in Seattle she had dreamed of being held like this by Cameron.

"Cameron," she whispered as the kiss ended. She reached out and ran her finger along his rugged jawline. She felt the slight roughness of his half a day's stubble.

"I've been wanting to do that since you came back to town," he murmured.

"What took you so long?" she teased.

"I have no idea," he said with a laid-back grin. "Maybe I was just waiting for the right time. I guess that I have to learn to make my own moments."

They walked around the festival in companionable

silence, the sort where it felt natural to not have to fill up the quiet with mindless chatter. Every now and again Cameron would point something out to look at or participate in. Paige shouldn't have been surprised when he began racking up stuffed-animal prizes for Emma.

Although she was having a relaxed, enjoyable outing, her thoughts kept drifting to the next town hall meeting, which was scheduled for the following day.

"What's this little frown for?" Cameron asked, reaching out to smooth away a crease between her eyes.

"I'm a little nervous about tomorrow evening," she admitted. It was her last chance to speak about the cannery before the vote next week. If the proposal didn't pass the vote, it would feel like a personal rejection of her and everything she was fighting for in Love.

"You've got this. There's nothing to worry about. The whole town is buzzing about what a cannery would mean to our economy. It's almost as if everyone is daring to hope again for prosperity." Cameron grinned at her. She couldn't look away from the way the corners of his mouth crinkled when he smiled. "And everyone thinks it was mighty brave of you to come back to Love."

Paige ducked her head down. She felt a bit embarrassed by the idea of people praising her. She hadn't done a single thing yet other than return money that should never have been taken in the first place.

She shook her head, pushing back strands of hair that had wandered in front of her eyes. "It's hard to accept kudos for simply doing the right thing."

"You're pretty extraordinary. After your history with

this community it's amazing that you're so committed to its recovery."

Paige studied Cameron's awestruck expression. "You forget that this is my hometown, too. I may not have been born here, but for many years it was my haven."

"I didn't forget. I'm just overwhelmed by your grace. Don't take this the wrong way, but you've changed. You're so grounded in your faith and your principles."

Paige smiled in acknowledgment. "Yes, I have changed. Being a mother will do that to a woman. My relationship with God has given me a new perspective. A lot of things make sense now. When my father passed, I drew to Him for strength." She met his gaze, moved by the compassion and understanding etched on Cameron's face. "I was at rock bottom when I left here. I was spiritually bankrupt for many years. It's amazing what can happen when you surrender yourself to God and seek a faith-driven life. Everything becomes much clearer."

"It's sort of like having smudgy glasses and then getting a new pair," Cameron said. "The whole world starts to look spanking new."

Paige burst out laughing. "That's a great way to describe it."

Cameron looked down. All of a sudden his expression changed from lighthearted to somber. "I'm sorry you had to go through it all by yourself. The pregnancy. Emma's birth. Raising her as a single mother. I'm sure it wasn't easy."

Immediately she bristled. "Don't feel bad for me. I made the choice to go it alone. It didn't break me."

And despite everything, she had built a happy home for Emma.

"I don't pity you. To be honest, I'm wishing that I had been at the hospital when Emma came into the world and took her first breath. I would have liked to cut her umbilical cord and to have learned how to change her diaper. But I'm very grateful that she had a mother like you who's been with her every step of the way. Just watching her for a few hours the other day gave me a whole new appreciation for all your sacrifices and loving care."

"Sorry if I snapped at you," Paige said with a rueful twist of her mouth. "That subject is a little prickly for me. Back in Seattle a lot of people looked down on me being a single mother raising a child on her own. Lots of prying eyes and endless questions. Even some preaching from members of my faith community. It taught me a huge lesson about judgment."

"It's no one's job to criticize you," Cameron said in a curt voice. "Thankfully, God's forgiveness allows us to move forward without being beaten up or condemned over our choices."

All of a sudden Hazel walked up, holding tightly on to Aidan's hand while Jasper pushed Emma in the carriage. Paige couldn't help but grin at the sight of the crotchety mayor of Love pushing a stroller. She saw Cameron's lips twitching with laughter and she had to look away before she dissolved into giggles.

Little beads of sweat were pooled on his forehead. "All this walking has me hotter than the Sahara Desert," Jasper grumbled as he fanned himself.

"Why don't I go get us some lemonade," Paige suggested. "That will cool everyone off."

"Oh, I'd love one," Hazel said. "I'm pretty parched."

"Need some help?" Cameron asked.

She waved him off. "I'll be fine. Why don't you stay here with your daughter?"

It was amazing how good it felt to refer to Emma as Cameron's daughter. And it didn't escape her notice the way his face lit up with joy upon hearing her say it. She felt a pang remembering what he'd said about wishing he had been a part of Emma's earliest moments. If she had to do it all over again, she would make different choices. She should never have withheld her pregnancy from him. But she couldn't go back. Only forward.

Just as she reached the lemonade concession stand, she heard someone calling out to her.

"Paige." She turned around at the mention of her name. Dwight was standing there with an intense look etched on his face.

After the way he'd reacted to her at the town meeting, she felt very skeptical about anything he had to say to her. She sincerely hoped he wasn't about to lay into her about the cannery proposal.

"Hello, Dwight," she said in a cool voice.

"I was hoping to see you here today. I have something for you." He shoved a manila packet in her hands. "Don't worry. It doesn't bite," he said with a smirk.

"What is this?" Paige asked. At the town meeting he'd made it clear that he didn't approve of her bid to resurrect the cannery project. She wasn't naive enough to think that he was trying to help her.

"Information that might change your mind about the cannery deal," he said cryptically.

"And why would I do that?" she snapped.

"Because things don't stay the same, Paige. Two years ago there wasn't another cannery in this particular area of Alaska." He shook his head. "A long time has passed since this deal was in the works. That's a lifetime in the business world. Things move at the speed of light. I did some research. Three canneries have been opened during that time. Three! Two of them are doing quite well, while the third one is struggling. Rumor has it they might file for Chapter 11 bankruptcy."

Three canneries? She hadn't known that. Why hadn't she known that? She had done some research but clearly nothing as comprehensive as Dwight's inquiry.

"Do you have any idea how difficult it would be for us to compete against two other canneries that are already established?"

Although Dwight was the furthest thing from warm and fuzzy, his words had been heartfelt and to the point. This move didn't reek of manipulation. There was something very authentic about it. Dwight adored his hometown and he didn't want to see the town's finances run off the rails again. And neither did she. She swallowed past the huge lump in her throat. Truth. That was what she had been fighting for ever since her father had stolen the town's funds. And now, out of the blue, it was being handed to her on a silver platter from the most unlikely of sources.

"I understand," she said with a nod of her head. "It

might be risky to open a cannery here after those other outfits are already up and running successfully."

But after everything she had endured, it was difficult to just give up on the dream. Maybe Dwight was wrong. "On the other hand, perhaps Love could do it better than those other two. There's no need for doom and gloom." She held her chin up even though she was trembling with doubt.

Dwight narrowed his gaze. "Or this town could lose a big chunk of money chasing a pipe dream. You seem to have a lot of pull here despite what happened with your father. You came back with your adorable daughter and the tragic news about your father. That could sway a lot of people to vote for a cannery project that isn't a smart business decision. Plus, you seem to have the Prescott family in your back pocket," he grumbled.

"The townsfolk are savvy enough to make their own decisions," she pointed out.

Dwight held up his hands. "My job here is done. The data I gave you is worth looking at before the upcoming vote. Don't say I didn't warn you."

He turned on his heel and walked away, leaving her reeling with the ramifications of the information he had just shared with her. She took the envelope and folded it into a small square, then stuffed it into her purse. As she purchased the lemonade and walked back toward the rides to meet up with Cameron and Emma, her mind whirled with the impact of her run-in with Dwight.

With another town meeting scheduled for tomorrow in preparation for next week's vote, she had no idea what to do in order to best serve the town she loved. The responsibility was weighing heavily on her. At the moment the stakes really couldn't get any higher.

Chapter Ten

Bright and early the next morning Cameron was serving customers at the Moose Café and whistling as he worked. He was still feeling content after the fun-filled day spent at the spring festival. The kiss he had shared with Paige had been tender and unforgettable. If he closed his eyes, he could almost feel the softness of her lips. Something hopeful had been in the air between them and he sensed that Paige had felt it also.

Was this a sign of new beginnings?

After such a long time of stuffing his feelings down, it was freeing to actually be hopeful about having a future with Paige. And he couldn't even describe how it had felt to be a family unit yesterday with Emma by their side. He had to believe that in bringing them to Love, God had been shining a light on the path He wanted him to take.

"You seem happier than a hummingbird in flight," Sophie said as he walked into the kitchen whistling an upbeat tune.

"It's going to be a good day, Sophie. I can feel it," he said. And he could—all the way down to his bones. He felt as if a powerful, sweet change was blowing in the wind. And he couldn't wait to see what bloomed as a result.

The energy surrounding tonight's town meeting had reached a fever pitch. Most folks in town seemed invigorated by the possibility of Love moving forward to reinvent itself.

Sophie grinned at him, showcasing her girl-next-door smile. "I sometimes have feelings like that, too. Good vibrations, I call 'em."

"Good vibrations. I like that," Cameron said.

Yes, indeed. Things were turning around. Not only for the community but for him, as well. His life was different since Paige had returned. He'd been enriched by Emma. His little girl made him think of the future and how he could shape it for good. It wasn't enough to sit on the sidelines and hope for the best. He'd given up on that front after the cannery fiasco, but he was committed to making Love prosperous again. Paige had forced him to recognize his own pride and blindness. And judgment. Never again in his life did he want to falsely tarnish the character of another human being. Particularly someone he adored.

Although the knowledge of his colossal error had been working its way through him ever since Paige's return, he'd resisted taking stock of everything. It was painful to realize that he'd been so terribly wrong about this woman who had been his first and only love. Emma's mother. A woman he had wanted to make his bride.

Two years ago he'd lacked the courage to stand up for Paige amid all the accusations lodged against her. His devotion to her hadn't been strong enough to silence the doubts. And now Cameron could see even more amazing sides to Paige Reynolds. And when he added up all the pieces, her innocence shone through like a beacon. He couldn't turn back time and undo the damage, no matter how fervently he wished it were possible. But he could move forward and humbly apologize to Paige. He could try to make amends.

"Cameron. Can you help me with these drinks? I'm getting a little backed up," Sophie said as she placed two orders on separate trays.

"Sure thing. I'll follow right behind you."

"Let me get the door for you," Hazel said, moving ahead of them so she could help out.

Sophie sailed through the door with Cameron following right behind her. All of a sudden she stopped in her tracks, causing Cameron to nearly lose his balance and the drinks he was holding.

"Hey. Watch it, Sophie. That was a close one," he said.

"Look, y'all. Gunther is on his knees," Sophie shrieked.

Gunther Reid was a regular customer at the Moose Café. Born and bred in Love, he'd been a friend of his since they were kids in the schoolyard. Affable and honorable, Gunther was the kind of person you rooted for.

Sure enough, when Cameron looked over at his pal's usual table, he was on bended knee.

"I'm about to swoon," Sophie gushed. "They are so inspiring."

Everything was hushed and still in the eatery. All eyes were on Gunther.

"This is where we had our very first date," Gunther said. A huge smile was plastered on his face as he gazed up at his beloved, Wanda. "It's a fitting place to ask you to spend the rest of your life with me and make me the happiest man in Alaska."

"Just Alaska?" Cameron muttered, earning him an outraged frown from Sophie.

"Shh," she said, placing her finger on her lips.

Wanda let out a scream of delight. "Oh, Gunther. Yes! Yes! Of course I'll marry you." She swooped down and wrapped her arms around Gunther's neck.

"W-Wanda. C-can't breathe."

"Oh, sweetie, I'm so sorry," she said, releasing Gunther's neck from her grip.

Gunther reached into his pocket, pulled out a wooden box and popped it open. "It's not the fanciest of rings, but it's straight from the heart."

The simple solitaire diamond shimmered and glinted from inside the box. Tears gathered in Wanda's eyes. "Oh, it's stunning. Please put it on my finger so I'll know I'm not dreaming."

She held out her hand and Gunther took the ring and gently placed it on Wanda's finger.

It was almost as if all the diners in the café had been holding their breath during the proposal. Once it became official, loud applause rang out in the room.

"Wait till Jasper finds out," Hazel said. "He's keeping a tally of all the engagements that occur as a result of Operation Love. Not sure what we're up to now, but Jasper's program really is working."

"Happy endings and all," Sophie chirped. "I sure hope mine is finding its way toward me."

Happy endings. Seeing Gunther and Wanda so ecstatic over their engagement was an awesome moment to witness. Before Wanda came to Love under the Operation Love program, Gunther had been a lonely bachelor. He had been shy and reserved. A bit of a homebody. Falling in love with sociable Wanda had forced him out of his shell. He had been the first one in line to court her when she had arrived in town. From the very beginning, Gunther had known Wanda was his one true love.

His one true love was Paige. It always had been. And he didn't have a single reason now not to pursue his own happy ending. So what if his parents hadn't gone the distance? That shouldn't define his own future. It didn't mean he couldn't make things work with Paige.

For far too long pride and circumstances had been stumbling blocks in their relationship. For two long years they hadn't been in each other's lives. They had both changed for the better in the past few years. Leading faith-driven lives had given them more purpose and a spiritual focus. He didn't think he would ever make the same mistakes with Paige that he had made in the past. Not many people were allowed a second opportunity to get things right.

Tonight after the town hall meeting, he planned to make a huge declaration to Paige, one that would hopefully change their relationship forever. He prayed that she still had feelings for him and was open to exploring a life together. If need be, he'd get on his knees and apologize to her for all the suspicions he'd harbored in his heart against her. For all the time they'd wasted.

Cameron stood at a distance and watched Gunther and Wanda as they celebrated their engagement with two frozen caramel mochaccinos. A feeling of excitement mixed with raw nerves rushed through him. He was ready to fight for his own happily-ever-after.

By six o'clock Paige was a bundle of jitters. Her palms were moist and a huge lump had settled in her throat. So much was riding on tonight's meeting. Love's prosperity was hanging in the balance. After reaching out to Grace last night, she had felt more reassured about the path she needed to take. Hours of brainstorming and prayer had helped her sort everything out. Before any vote took place next week, she needed to address the residents. She had no idea if her words would be well received, considering her history, but she was convinced that if things went her way, the town would be heading in the right direction.

In stark contrast to the last time she'd walked the gauntlet toward the town council's meeting room, this time she was stopped by dozens of well-wishers. Some folks congratulated her for being dedicated to the cannery project, while others asked her about Emma and thanked her for returning the money to Love. Although it felt nice to be greeted so warmly, she couldn't help but wonder how everyone would react to her change of heart.

Paige had made a point to get to town hall just as the

meeting started so she wouldn't have to sit by Cameron. By not telling him about her encounter with Dwight and the information he had shared with her, she felt as if she had hidden something from him. He'd been so supportive of her desire to achieve redemption for her father and revitalize the cannery project. Because of the way she felt about Cameron, she knew he might be able to sway her opinion. And she hadn't wanted to make her decision based on what someone else thought. Love's financial recovery had been her only focus.

Cameron shot her a quizzical look as she settled in a few rows behind him rather than joining him. She nodded in his direction, then looked away. It was better this way, she realized. She needed to keep her eyes on the prize and concentrate on the reason she was here tonight. Her feelings for him had never done anything but lead her astray.

Paige sat through the meeting and waited for the perfect opening to say her piece.

Just as Jasper began to talk about voting, she stood up. She cleared her throat. "Jasper. I'd like to share a few thoughts before we get started tonight. I'll try to be brief."

Jasper peered at her over his spectacles. His expression reflected his impatience. "Go ahead and say your piece, but we've got a long agenda to get through. Keep it short and sweet, just like my baby granddaughter."

For once Dwight didn't seem to have an objection to her taking the floor and addressing the townsfolk. He eyed her with simple curiosity.

Her walk to the front of the room felt like an endless

march. With a steadying breath, she faced the crowded-to-capacity room, twiddling her fingers in front of her to relieve some tension.

Please, Lord, let the words flow easily from my lips so that I can present this in the best way possible. I love this town so dearly, and I want to help them prosper.

"Good evening, everyone. I wasn't expecting to be up here tonight, but my conscience won't allow me to stay silent. Yesterday Dwight shared some information with me that changes my position on the cannery project."

Shocked gasps rang out along with a host of groans. People began grumbling and she could hear Dwight's name being murmured. They seemed upset. She held up her hand. "Please don't be upset with Dwight. He was acting as a dedicated steward of this town." She sent him a nod of acknowledgment. She wasn't sure if she was imagining it, but she was almost certain he smiled at her. Paige turned back toward the audience, making an effort not to lock gazes with Cameron. She could only imagine he was probably confused and hurt that she hadn't discussed this with him prior to tonight's meeting. But up until a few hours ago she hadn't been exactly sure of what she was going to say or do this evening. It had all come together at the last moment.

"There have been three canneries in the southeastern part of Alaska that have opened their doors in the last two years. I'll admit that I wasn't aware of that figure until yesterday. The last one that opened isn't doing very well, no doubt because of steep competition from the other two." She swung her gaze around the room.

"Why does that matter to us, you might ask? Because if the town decides to put a considerable amount of money into this project, it's important to consider the existing market. Knowing what I know at this moment, I think it's too risky. Could it be a success? Very possibly. But it's also likely that the cannery could go under. A few hours ago everything became crystal clear.

"For me the cannery project has always represented a lost opportunity. Its failure was a symbol of my father's sins and my own banishment from Love." She inhaled a deep breath. "I truly love this community and it's imperative that I do right by it. The success of this town can't be about my father's redemption. And it shouldn't be about things that have been lost. I tossed and turned last night trying to figure out what's in the best interest for Love. And it's not the cannery. I know that now. Jasper was right when he said it's about moving forward, not backward."

She looked straight at Cameron. His eyes glinted with disappointment before he turned his gaze away from her. In that single moment she feared she might have lost him forever. She paused for a second to steady herself against the pain ricocheting through her.

"So it sounds like we're right back where we started from," someone in the audience called out.

"No, actually, we're not," Paige responded in a firm voice. "Far from it, in fact. Hazel's boots are a far better investment than a cannery, considering the unique marketing slant and the freshness of the idea. There are no other shoes on the market that can claim to be authentic Alaskan-made boots. And the unfinished cannery building could easily be converted into a production facility for the boots. If we scale back the scope of the building, it could be finished in a matter of months—weeks, even, since we have extended hours of sunlight now."

She glanced over at Grace, who had promised to sit near the front row so she could be available to speak. "Grace, could you help me out with this part?" Her call to Grace last night had led to hours of discussion, during which Boone's wife had acted as a sounding board and helped her analyze the benefits of a cannery versus a shoemaking enterprise. In the end, her assistance had been invaluable.

Grace came up and stood next to her. "The money Paige returned to the town could easily be used to jumpstart this new business. We've already been working on a cost analysis for the launch, and these additional funds could really assist in establishing Hazel's boots. It's an amazing opportunity to truly put our resources behind what could be a huge revenue stream for this town."

"I love it!" Hazel cried out, thumping her palm down on the dais. She paused to swipe away a few tears. "It's a brilliant plan, as far as I'm concerned."

"Wow," Boone said, scratching his jaw. "Put the two of you together and you could achieve world peace." Grace blew her husband a kiss.

"We're going to need a name for this enterprise. We can't keep calling it 'Hazel's boots,' unless that's really the name for it," Declan said.

Hazel vehemently shook her head. "Nope. I don't

need 'em named after me. Let's think of something else. Something that makes 'em stand up and take notice."

Suddenly everyone started calling out suggestions. Operation Love. Nothing but Love. Made in Love. Alaska's Own. Love's Boots.

"Hush, everyone. Plenty of time to figure that out later on," Jasper said in a cranky tone. "If we're not voting next week on the cannery project, I need to make a motion to that effect. I hereby move that we scrap the proposed vote for the cannery project."

"I second it," Dwight said.

"Motion carries," Jasper said with a bang of his gavel.

"I hereby move that at next month's meeting we vote on making the cannery building the new site for production and operations of Hazel's boots," Boone said.

"Second!" Hazel shouted gleefully.

"Motion carries," Jasper said with another pounding of his gavel.

Paige felt a warm, settled feeling in her chest. All was well within her heart and mind. She hadn't done the easy thing, but in the end, it had been the right thing. For so long she had been focused on the goal of having a cannery open up its doors in Love. It had seemed to be the perfect way to erase the pain of the past few years. She had wanted desperately to restore what her father tore down. But now, by truly putting the past behind them, the town could soar with this new idea.

By the time Jasper adjourned the meeting forty-five minutes later, Paige was desperate to smooth things over with Cameron. The expression he'd had on his face during her speech worried her. If nothing else, she didn't want to lose the friendship they had been fostering over the past few weeks. It was crucial for Emma's well-being.

Although she tried to get to Cameron, she found herself staring after him as she became the center of a throng of well-wishers.

Look at me. Just give me one little look, she silently urged him.

Instead of glancing in her direction, he seemed to be caught up in his own thoughts. A dejected look was etched on his face.

"Cameron!" she called out, catching up to him just as he was about to exit the room. His expression was shuttered.

"Good evening," he said with a nod. "You're full of surprises tonight."

"I'm sorry that I didn't give you a heads-up. It all came together so quickly." She rushed the words out, anxious about his reaction.

"No problem, Paige." His mouth quirked. "Everything worked out beautifully."

"I think Hazel's boots will serve this town well."

"Congratulations. From the sounds of it, you got everything you wanted. Just one question. Does this mean you're going to be heading back to Seattle?"

The question was thrown at her the way a pitcher might throw a curveball. She hadn't expected to have to answer a question like this tonight. Especially not from Cameron.

"I've built a life for Emma and myself in Seattle. It only makes sense that we go back home," she said.

For a moment Cameron looked as if someone had punched him in the gut. Pain flickered in his eyes and she knew without a single doubt that he was thinking about Emma.

"Cameron, we can work out a schedule. You'll always be in Emma's life. You're her father," she said in a low voice. "It will all work out."

She was winging it now, saying the mature things that a mother should say in a situation like this. The reality was that she didn't want to leave Love, but it was hard to justify staying here in town without a purpose. And to stay here with the shadow of her relationship with Cameron always hanging over her head wasn't something she could do. Not when she'd fallen in love with him all over again.

Raw emotions flitted across his face. His expression hardened. "I never wanted to be a long-distance father, Paige. Take it from my own experience—sometimes it doesn't all work out."

Without saying another word, he turned and disappeared through the door, leaving Paige feeling crestfallen.

She hadn't wanted to hurt him or to revive memories of his own parental abandonment. She'd come all the way to Love so that he could meet Emma and forge a bond with her. Over the past few weeks the father-daughter duo had done just that. Cameron clearly adored their baby girl. And he now occupied a tender place in Emma's world that no one else could ever assume. She had grown to love him and even learned to call him Dada. But what if Cameron allowed anger and bitterness to get in the way of his relationship with Emma? He'd once decided that he no longer needed Paige in his world. He'd cast her out of his life without sparing her a second thought. What if it happened again? Only this time around she wouldn't be the only one he wounded.

Even though she had tried to guard herself against falling in love with Cameron, Paige hadn't been able to stop herself. Being in his warm, steady presence had made it easy for her to forget how badly he'd hurt her in the past. And recently she had begun to imagine how sweet life could be if they could only repair the pain of their past and dedicate themselves to one another and Emma as a family.

Tears misted in her eyes as the realization hit her that it wasn't meant to be. Once again Cameron was showing her how easy it was for him to walk away from her without hashing out their issues.

Nursing her broken heart the first time around had been agonizing. This time might just break her into little pieces.

Yes, indeed. It was safe to say he was moping. He had been sitting there like a fool when Paige had dropped the bombshell that she was no longer pushing for the cannery project. He let out a harsh laugh. So much for her calling him her ally. So much for her considering how it would feel for him to be blindsided. And his fears had been realized this evening when she'd admitted that she was heading back to Seattle with his little girl.

Humph! She had always been good at pulling the rug out from under him!

She hadn't even given him the courtesy of a heads-up. Yet she'd brainstormed with Grace, whom she barely knew. That simple fact had added insult to injury. Despite the progress he'd thought they had made since Paige's return, she'd still seen fit to keep him in the dark. Some things never changed.

He felt sick to his stomach. A cannery project would have kept Paige and Emma in Love. He had heard her say it with his own ears. But according to Paige, she wouldn't be sticking around in town now that everything had been wrapped up with a nice little bow. Paige's speech had almost sounded like a goodbye. After all, as long as Love was able to grow and prosper with the money she'd returned, her mission would be fulfilled.

Redemption accomplished.

The thought of Paige leaving town again gutted him. It had been agonizing the first time around, but now it would be unbearable. She would be taking a pint-size version of him along with her. His beautiful daughter, who was surely the best part of him.

Why hadn't he pulled her aside and laid it all on the line as Hazel and Boone had suggested? Why hadn't he told her how he really felt? Why was he always running away when emotions ran high?

He was head over heels in love with Paige. That knowledge had always been there, safely nestled in his heart and tucked away where it couldn't cause him any more heartache. But despite what he had done to protect himself, he was in pain now, broken by the harsh reality of his situation. If he kept silent and said nothing, he was certain to lose her. But if he pushed past all the doubts and fears and confessed his love to Paige, there was always the possibility of suffering a huge rejection. He wasn't sure he could handle that.

By the time he reached his house, Cameron was emotionally fatigued and exhausted. When he opened his front door and walked in, he heard a rustling sound. Looking down, he noticed a long white envelope sitting on the hardwood floor. He crouched down and picked it up, his body stiffening at the swirly, unique handwriting. The letter was from Robert. Paige must have delivered it to his house earlier today. Adrenaline raced through his body as he contemplated whether or not he even wanted to read Robert's parting words.

He sighed. How many times was he going to run away from the things that challenged him? The things that reached into his chest cavity and tugged at him? He opened the envelope with his finger and pulled out the letter. He felt a lump in his throat as he began to read the letter.

Dear Cameron,
By the time you read this letter, I will no longer be on earth, but in Heaven with the Lord.

I deeply regret how my actions tainted you and destroyed your relationship with Paige.

Mere words could never capture how deeply I wish I had been a better man.

God has forgiven me for my weakness, even though I haven't managed to forgive myself. You were the son I never had, Cam. And hopefully you will someday be Paige's husband. The two of you belong together. Please don't let my sins affect your future. Your beautiful Emma deserves a family. The type of family you can build with my beloved daughter. Remember…tomorrow is promised to no man. Live with love while you can.

With love and regret,

Robert

Cameron let out a ragged sigh as he finished the letter, folded it in half and put it back in its envelope. He brushed a tear away. The missive couldn't have come at a better time. Knowing that Robert had truly been remorseful provided the closure he so desperately needed. And hearing his old friend confirm his own thoughts about creating a family with Paige and Emma showed him that he was on the right path.

Like Robert had said, tomorrows were never promised. He was going to reach out and grab his happiness, not only for himself, but for Paige and Emma, as well.

If he kept quiet, he stood to lose everything he held so dear. What kind of man would he be if he walked that same path yet again? As a father, how could he ever look Emma in the eye and tell her that he'd done his best to keep their family together? Becoming a man of God meant stepping out on a limb and believing. Hoping. Praying.

With faith, hope and love, everything was possible. Instead of dwelling on how complicated his world had become, he needed to simplify everything. He needed to go to Paige and lay himself and his feelings bare before her. Like never before, he began to pray. He prayed that somewhere in her heart Paige still loved him. He prayed that he would find the words to convey the depth and breadth of his feelings. He prayed that it wasn't too late to make things right and keep his family together.

Chapter Eleven

By the time Paige made it back to the homestead, she was just in time to put Emma down for the night. Even though she was a bit fussy, Paige managed to rock her to sleep. Although she felt at peace with regards to the resolution of the cannery project, thoughts of Cameron continued to run through her mind. Perhaps she should have chased after him in an attempt to smooth things over? Fear had held her back. Despite how far they had come, she still worried about making herself vulnerable.

If she was being honest with herself, all signs lately had pointed to a possible reconciliation for the two of them. He had been so tender toward her. And that wonderful kiss they had shared loomed large in her thoughts. It had been so full of hope and promise for a new beginning. But it hadn't come to pass. Perhaps their painful history was too powerful to overcome.

The sound of tires crunching in her driveway drew her attention to the window. The outside light illuminated a truck that resembled the one Cameron drove.

With her pulse racing, she watched as he stepped down from the pickup and began walking toward her front door. Not wanting the doorbell to awaken Emma, Paige pulled it open to greet him.

Looking a bit weary, Cameron stood on her stoop dressed in the same casual outfit he had worn earlier at the meeting. His rugged, strong presence was overwhelming.

"Cameron. I'm surprised to see you here. Is everything all right?"

"Everything's fine. There's no emergency," he said. "May I come in?"

"Of course," she said, opening the door wide and ushering him inside.

Cameron turned toward her. There was a strained edge to his features. He seemed jittery.

"I left the meeting rather abruptly. And I was short with you. Rude, even. I'm really sorry about that."

Paige nodded, feeling relieved that he'd addressed the elephant in the room. "I understand. Things were so hectic afterward and I know you must have wondered why I didn't talk to you about the information Dwight gave me."

"I'd be lying if I said it didn't bother me," Cameron admitted. "I would like to think you could tell me anything. But, more important, I've been wrangling for weeks now with something that I need to get off my chest."

Paige frowned. "What is it?"

"I'm ashamed about my blindness. All this time I've been holding on to the past when I should have been moving toward the future. I was wrong about you, Paige. I know you had nothing to do with your father's embezzling from the town funds."

She felt a heavy weight being lifted from her chest as Cameron spoke the words she'd been waiting to hear for two years. "H-how? Why now?" she asked.

"I've been putting the pieces together for a while. When you told me about the trust fund, it was the first time there was an actual explanation for the money you'd been tossing around."

She shook her head. "I don't know why I didn't mention it all that time ago," she murmured. "I suppose that I didn't want you to view me as some pampered princess."

He let out a groan. "You shouldn't have had to, Paige. I was wrong in every way possible. My pride and anger and my history with my parents led me to think the very worst of you."

Paige's eyes pricked with tears. This moment had been years in the making. She had prayed about Cameron realizing he was wrong on numerous occasions.

The sound of Emma's cries rang out from upstairs. Paige turned in that direction, ready to run to check in on her. Normally she would hear Fiona's footsteps echoing from overhead as she walked the hardwood floors. This evening her nanny had taken ill and was resting comfortably in bed. Paige cocked her head to the side, listening for Emma's cries.

"Is she okay?" Cameron asked.

"She might have had a bad dream," Paige said. When

the screams continued, Paige said, "I need to go check in with her."

She quickly made her way up the staircase. Cameron was right behind her as she entered the nursery. She strode to the crib, where Emma was sitting up and howling. Her face was red and tear-streaked from crying. She was breathing heavily.

"What's wrong, sweetie?" Paige asked in a soft voice.

"Mama!" Emma cried.

"Oh, you're warm," Paige said, feeling slightly alarmed. Fiona also had a fever and they suspected she had come down with a virus.

Cameron reached out and touched Emma's forehead. "She's just a little warm. Why don't we give her some pain reliever and something cold to drink?"

Paige nodded and quickly began to mobilize. Cameron had been right. After taking her temperature, Paige realized that she had only a slight fever. A cold cloth, pain reliever and apple juice helped to soothe her. For the next few hours Cameron and Paige sat up with Emma and calmed her as best they could.

Paige watched as Cameron rocked Emma to sleep in his arms. A groundswell of emotion welled up inside her at the sight of the two of them so interconnected. She craved more quiet moments like this. It felt amazing to not have to parent all by herself. Cameron's strong, steady companionship was a blessing. With him in the picture, everything seemed sweeter and richer. It truly felt as if they were a family.

As she looked over at Cameron, then swung her gaze back to Emma, a single truth settled over her. For so many years she had been seeking a family. After her mother died, things had changed so drastically at home. And even though her father had grown to be a loving, engaged father, she had never again experienced that family dynamic. Until now. Until this very moment. Cameron and Emma were her home. Without the two of them, nothing really made sense in her world.

Once Emma was fast asleep, Cameron gently placed her down into the crib. For a few moments he stood next to the crib with Paige as they gazed down at her, listening to the light sounds of her breathing. There was nothing more precious in this whole world than their daughter. Paige resisted the urge to reach out and caress Emma's cheek. She didn't want to run the risk of waking her from her precious slumber. She looked so snug and secure wrapped up in the sheet and blanket. The only thing missing, Emma realized, was Lola Bear. As if he had read her mind, Cameron took the stuffed animal from the top of Emma's dresser and gently placed it down beside their child.

After a few minutes they made their way back downstairs, and Cameron turned to her and took her hands in his. He looked deep into her eyes, his expression intense. "I was wrong about you. You're strong. Honest. And in case I failed to mention it, you're a wonderful mother to our daughter. Emma is mighty fortunate to have a mom like you. You remind me of Alaskan fireweed. Despite the harsh climate, they persevere, bringing beauty wherever they're planted. Two years ago this town did you a disservice. I did you a disservice. We were wrong. Period. End of story. I just want to say that

I'm sorry about my role in it." He heaved a tremendous sigh. "Sometimes we lash out in our pain and shock and fear. That's what we did to you, Paige. And I want you to know I wish you had never been forced out of town. I don't want to dredge it all up again, but I couldn't let another day go by without apologizing."

Her vision blurred as moisture gathered in her eyes. She had never dared to dream about being absolved of all guilt by Cameron. Or getting a sincere apology from him. Not after everything her father's greed had cost his beloved town. It meant everything to her to hear his supportive words.

She sniffed back tears. This night had been full of emotion. "You're going to make me cry. I'm going to be a sniveling mess."

He reached out and ran his palm over her cheek. "There's nothing wrong with tears. Don't ever be afraid to show your humanity. Without it, we're nothing. The letter from your father drove that point home to me. Thank you for making sure I received it."

She wiped away the wetness from her cheek. "I'm so happy it was meaningful to you. He loved you, Cam. Despite everything he did, I think he wanted the best for both of us."

Cameron nodded, his expression reflective. "Paige, I need to ask you a favor. Could you meet me over at the Moose Café tomorrow afternoon? Around two o'clock?"

A favor? "Sure. Unless Emma is still not feeling well. I expect her to be fine, though. She barely had a temperature."

The glint in Cameron's eyes hinted at things she

wasn't sure it was wise to believe in. "Great. You should get some rest, Paige. It's getting late. I'll see you to-morrow."

The moment Cameron left the homestead, Paige immediately felt the loss of him being at her side. For so long she had weathered parenthood alone. It felt so nice to share it with someone—the hardships, the joy, the small triumphs. Watching Cameron have such a calming effect on Emma as he crooned her a lullaby had been powerful. If she hadn't already been in love with him, it would have made her tumble right over the edge.

But she was already madly, deeply, forever in love with Emma's daddy. And although it was a scary feeling, she also felt triumphant and centered. It was pretty amazing to still experience those feelings after separation, turmoil and despair. And if nothing ever came of her feelings for Cameron, she still felt fortunate to have experienced them.

Hope still flourished in her heart for a happy ending. The future was stretched out before them with so much potential for joy and poignant moments. Paige hoped Cameron realized that it was never too late for new beginnings.

As the sun crept over the horizon, a fully restored Emma woke up ready to take the world by storm. Paige chuckled to herself as she listened to her over the baby monitor. She was giggling and talking to herself. The thermometer verified that she no longer had even the slightest of temperatures. Cameron had called to check in on Emma, endearing him even more to Paige. There had been so much love and concern in his voice it gave her goose bumps.

At quarter to two she settled Emma into her car seat and headed into town. She felt her heart constrict as she passed by the pier and the fishing boats, as well as all the quaint shops on Jarvis Street. How she would miss this fishing village she loved so dearly. Seattle had been a great place to live, yet it had never felt like home.

As soon as she entered the Moose Café, enticing aromas drifted in her direction. Her stomach grumbled at the temptation. She and Emma were heartily greeted by several townsfolk. Although a few people still snubbed her, she considered it incredible progress.

As she walked past a table, she noticed Declan sitting down with five women surrounding him. The expression on his face was one of supreme boredom. She let out a chuckle as he spotted her and waved her over to the table.

"Hey, Paige. Hi, Emma. Why don't you come join us," he called out. His face looked anything but relaxed. The woman seated to his right was clutching his arm.

"Morning, Declan. Ladies," she said in a cheery voice.

Declan disentangled himself, then jumped up quickly and moved toward her. With his back to the table, Declan began making wild eye motions. He mouthed the words *Help me*.

Paige shook her head. "You're on your own," she said in a low voice.

He shook his head violently. "I know being sought after by five women might sound like every man's dream, but trust me, it's quickly becoming a nightmare. They won't give me a moment's peace."

"Just think of how happy Jasper will be if you end up hitting it off with one of them," she teased. "He might just throw you and your bride a fabulous Alaskan wedding." With a wave of her hand and a grin, she walked away and toward Hazel, leaving him with a dumbfounded expression on his face.

"Hi, Hazel," Paige said as she approached her at the coffee counter. "Is Cameron around? He told me to meet him here."

"Hey, girls. Cameron was in the back making some sort of specialty drink last time I checked." She let out a hearty laugh. "He loves coming up with new concoctions."

Emma immediately squirmed in her arms to get to Hazel. If Paige hadn't thought it was so cute, she might have been insulted by Emma wanting to ditch her for Hazel's arms. Bless her charming daughter. She firmly believed that if not for Emma, she might not have made as many inroads with the townsfolk upon her return to Love. It seemed that no one could resist a chubby-cheeked, green-hazel-eyed baby girl.

"How is my little cutie?" Hazel asked as she came out from behind the counter. She swung Emma up, then placed her against her chest. "Cameron told me about Emma not feeling well last night. I would have been there in a flash if you guys had needed me."

"Thanks for saying so. She's doing really well this morning. In a strange way it's almost as if it never happened, at least in Emma's world." Paige felt relieved that it was nothing more than a passing thing. She was already back to her usual self with no signs of not being well.

Hazel beamed as she looked at the little girl. "She's blessed. We all are. Having this Little Miss Sunshine in our lives makes everything brighter."

"Hey, would you mind watching her for a little bit? I'm going to go look for Cameron out back."

"Take your time. Lots of single men in town are at the café this morning." She winked at Paige. "I'm hoping Sophie finds her a fella. She deserves to find her happily-ever-after, just like you do, Paige."

"Well, we can't all be as fortunate as you and Jasper," she demurred. She had the feeling that Hazel was throwing out a hint about her relationship with Cameron, but she wasn't biting. "I promise to be quick. Give a shout if she's too much of a handful."

Paige walked toward the back. Along the way she took a moment to admire all that Cameron had built for himself with the café. It was such a cozy, warm place. It exuded charm. All the customers seemed happy and well taken care of by the staff. Cameron had been right. Some dreams couldn't be denied. She walked into the kitchen and immediately saw him fiddling around with a blender. He must have heard her coming, because he swung his gaze up to her and gifted her with a gorgeous smile. He placed the blender down and walked toward her, quickly swallowing up the space between them.

"Hey, Paige. Thanks for coming over."

"Of course. It sounded important. Emma is in front with Hazel." She ran her fingers through her hair. The way he was staring at her was making her nervous. She couldn't help but wonder if something was wrong.

"What's up, Cameron? Has something happened?" she asked, her nerves suddenly on edge.

He reached out and grabbed her hand. "Paige, I can't let another day go by without saying things to you that I should have said a long time ago."

Suddenly Paige saw a glimmer of something in his eyes that caused her to hope as she hadn't allowed herself to hope for a very long time.

Chapter Twelve

Cameron took a few steps toward her so that no gap existed between them.

"'Where you go I will go. Where you stay I will stay.'" The tenderness in Cameron's voice as he recited the Bible passage from Ruth threatened every ounce of her composure.

Little did Cameron know that it was one of her favorite Bible passages. It spoke to her, for a dozen different reasons.

"If you're determined to go back to Seattle, I'm coming with you. I wanted to bring you here to the Moose Café to tell you so that you will never doubt that you and Emma are the most important things in my world. Way more important than this place that I love."

One look at Cameron's expression showed her he was serious.

Paige shook her head. Disbelief roared through her. "Seattle? You're coming with us to Seattle?"

He reached out and placed both hands on either side

of her face. "I can live without many things, Paige, but you and Emma are as important to me as the air I breathe. So I'm packing up all my belongings and coming with the two of you. I'll leave it all behind. The Moose Café. My house. My truck. I'll miss my family like crazy, but I can always visit. That's what planes are for, right?" He let out a shaky laugh.

She took a step away from him. "Cameron, please don't say this for Emma's sake. What she needs most is stability, not two parents who are together simply out of duty and obligation."

He moved toward her, quickly bridging the gap between them. He reached out and cupped her face in his hands. He dipped his head down and captured her lips in a stunning, powerful kiss that left her breathless. It nearly knocked her off her feet because the kiss radiated love. It was something you couldn't fake or manufacture. The kiss said it all. Cameron was in love with her!

"I love you, Paige Reynolds. I always have. I always will. Two years ago I made the most foolish decision of my life. Despite everything I knew about you, I chose to believe the worst of you. I chose not to support the woman I loved. And that decision has cast a shadow over me ever since." He leaned down and brushed a kiss across Paige's forehead. "When you came back to Love with a big fat check for the town, I thought that was the biggest gift you could bestow on us. I still couldn't see the forest for the trees." Tears shone in his eyes. "Until I saw Emma. Until I realized that you gave me something even more precious. And ever since your return, you've been fighting for this town. To make things right.

To fulfill your father's dying wish. I don't think I've ever seen a person act with so much love in their heart."

A tremor ran across his jaw. "Every single thing you've done has been for the benefit of others. Emma. Robert's dying wish. Me. And this town. You have given unselfishly."

"Love has always been my home, Cameron. Deep down I think that I was hoping there would be a permanent place here for Emma and me."

"Of course there's a place for the two of you. And it's with me. You belong in Love, Paige, just as much as you belong wherever I am."

Tears slid down her face. "Oh, Cameron. God brought me back to Alaska. My heart led me straight back to you."

"I don't ever want to lose sight of the love we feel for one another. Having lost you once, I don't ever want to endure that hardship again. It's too painful."

"'Where you go I will go. Where you stay I will stay.'" Paige recited the verse solemnly. She meant it with every fiber of her being. A life lived without Cameron by her side would always feel incomplete. "And I've decided that Emma doesn't need a trust fund. She has the two of us—a family. I'm going to donate the money to a very worthy cause. This town we love so much."

Cameron's eyes went wide. "Are you sure? That's above and beyond." She nodded her head.

"Oh, Paige," Cameron said, placing a sweet kiss on her temple. "Jasper is going to do cartwheels when he finds out."

Paige laughed out loud and shook her head. "Let's hope not. This town needs the mayor in one piece."

"Two years ago I made a big mistake in forcing your hand. Instead of running after you and begging you to come back, I stuck my head in the sand and allowed pride and bitterness to consume me." He let out a hollow laugh. "Even then I loved you. Matter of fact, I can't remember a time when I wasn't in love with you. When you came walking back into my life, you turned me upside down. I wasn't ready to admit even to myself that I still had feelings for you. Part of me was still reeling from losing you the first time around. I didn't want to open myself up only to have a door closed on me."

"Oh, Cameron. I was wary, too. It broke my heart when I had to leave Alaska. And it tore me up inside to know that we would never have our happily-ever-after. Coming back wasn't supposed to be about our love story. It was supposed to be about Emma meeting her dad and fulfilling my father's wishes. But in the end, true love couldn't be denied."

"No, it can't. It perseveres despite the most challenging of circumstances." His voice was filled with awe.

Cameron lowered himself so that he was on bended knee. He looked up at Paige and winked. "I agree with you one hundred percent." He reached into his jacket pocket and pulled out a dark velvet box. "I had this ring made two and a half years ago for you." He made a face. "I was waiting for the perfect time to propose. Everything fell apart before I could find that moment. Needless to say, I'm mighty glad I held on to it."

Paige gasped as he flipped the box open. She raised her hand to her mouth. Her hands were trembling.

"I know you've always liked sapphires," Cameron said. "I hope you like it."

The stunning sapphire ring was surrounded by diamonds in a solitaire setting. It sparkled from inside the box. Paige had never seen a more spectacular ring in her life.

"I was foolish to ever let you walk out of my life." Tears shimmered in Cameron's eyes before a few slid down his face. Paige reached down and wiped them away. He smiled up at her.

"Paige, will you and Emma make me the happiest man in the world and marry me and be my family? I want nothing more than to build a life with you and our precious child, if you'll have me."

Paige felt as if her heart might just burst from sheer happiness. "Yes, Cameron," she said in a triumphant voice. "I love you. And nothing would make me happier than to commit myself to you before God and all our family and friends. Being a family is all I've ever wanted for us."

Cameron took the ring from the box and placed it on Paige's ring finger. "Family is everything. Without it, we're just hollow shells."

Paige nodded. "I wish we'd made our commitment to God and one another before we started our family, but I'm grateful for Emma and I am glad for His forgiveness."

Cameron stood up. "Emma was always in God's plan. And you and I were always meant to be together."

"And we will be," Paige said with a grin. "For the rest of our days."

Paige reached up and placed an exuberant kiss on Cameron's lips. He kissed her back, placing his hands around her waist and drawing her close.

"Forever," Cameron whispered against her lips as the joy they both felt about their magnificent future pulsed in the air around them.

Epilogue

The sun was shining brilliantly in a robin's-egg-colored sky. A light breeze swept over Paige and ruffled the hem of her lace-and-satin wedding gown. The melodic lilt of a harp filled the air. The smell of poppies wafted in the atmosphere. A feeling of joy swept over her. Her most cherished dream was about to come true. She had always wanted to be a June bride. And ever since she could remember, she had wanted to be Mrs. Cameron Prescott. She had dreamed of settling down with her husband and Emma right here in Love, Alaska. From this moment forward it would be her forever home.

She watched as Honor walked down the aisle as her maid of honor, holding tightly to Aidan's hand. After a sudden bout of shyness about his role in the wedding as ring bearer, he had insisted on walking beside Auntie Honor.

"Ready to get hitched?" Jasper asked with a wide grin. He held out his arm for her and she looped her own through his. She leaned over and placed a kiss on his grizzled cheek, filled with gratitude to him for standing in for her father.

"I've been waiting for this moment for a long time, Jasper," she said. "Wild horses couldn't stop me."

"Then let's get this train moving," Jasper said with a chuckle as they began to walk toward a waiting Cameron.

Everything seemed to be moving in slow motion as they walked down the aisle strewn with poppy petals. Her emotions were riding right on the surface as beloved friends and family members came into view. Dwight gave her a thumbs-up. Myrtle, looking fabulous in pelican pink, blew her a kiss. Sophie dabbed at her eyes with a tissue. Fiona was beaming with pride. The sight of Cameron standing at the altar with Emma in his arms caused a groundswell of emotion to rise up in her. He looked so distinguished in his wedding attire. Boone, Liam and Declan stood beside him as his groomsmen. And her sweet Emma looked so comfortable in her father's arms. By the grace of God, everything had turned out wonderfully. She couldn't have imagined a more perfect beginning to their life as husband and wife.

Once they reached the altar, Jasper handed her off with a gentlemanly flourish. She met Cameron's eyes, instantly seeing the promise of a lifetime in their depths. She loved this man to the core of her being. By allowing her to become Cameron's wife, God had bestowed on her the ultimate blessing. By giving her the courage to return to Love, He had shown her the power of forgiveness.

Hazel swept in and took Emma out of her father's arms. She went back to her seat and began bouncing the little girl on her lap. Emma made joyful little squeals.

"What took you so long?" Cameron asked in a low voice.

"I wanted to glide down the aisle with elegance, not trot like a horse," she teased.

"You were well worth the wait," Cameron said, leaning down and placing a tender kiss on her lips.

"You're not supposed to kiss her yet," Pastor Jack scolded with a shake of his head.

The wedding guests erupted into laughter.

"I was just practicing for later," Cameron said, his lips twitching with mirth.

As Pastor Jack conducted the wedding ceremony, Cameron and Paige exchanged vows and promised to honor each other with truth, love and fidelity for the rest of their days. There wasn't a dry eye among the guests.

"I now pronounce you husband and wife," Jack said with a wide grin.

"Can I kiss her now?" Cameron asked.

"If you didn't, I think Mrs. Prescott might have something to say about it," Jack teased, his face lit up with a brilliant smile.

"Mrs. Prescott," Paige said with a sigh. "That sounds wonderful."

Cameron leaned down and placed a triumphant kiss on his new bride's lips. With his hand on her lower back, he dipped her backward. Paige wrapped her arms around his neck and kissed him back, hanging on for dear life.

Cheers and shouts filled the air. Suddenly they were being bombarded with rose petals.

"You sure that you don't want to hop on a plane and disappear for a few days to a tropical island? Fiona said she'll be more than happy to watch Emma for us."

"No way! I'm finally home where I belong. This is the only place I want to be," she gushed.

"What a coincidence. Because I feel the exact same way, Mrs. Prescott."

Cameron leaned down and scooped Paige up into his arms and carried her back down the aisle to the hoots and cheers of all their family and friends. Emma began to trail after them, her chubby little face shining with the happiest of smiles.

Paige had never been more content in her life. She had found her bliss by returning to Alaska. Her most fervent wish had come true. She now had a real family with Cameron and Emma and the whole Prescott family. Redemption. Happily-ever-after.

And above all, the promise of a lifetime lived in Love.

* * * * *

Keep reading for an exclusive excerpt of
THE RAIN SPARROW by
New York Times *bestselling author Linda Goodnight.*
Available now from HQN Books!

Dear Reader,

Thank you for joining me on this voyage to Love, Alaska. I love reunion romances. There is something very reassuring to me about a love that never fades away despite the passage of time or circumstances. Paige and Cameron are two people who never stopped loving one another, despite a past littered with betrayal, pain and mistrust. Although they have obstacles to hurdle, the presence of their daughter, Emma, serves as motivation for them to shed the pain of the past and forge a new, shiny future.

Family is at the core of this story. Both Cameron and Paige want to give their daughter a family, yet both are afraid to get their hopes up. As a writer, there is something very poignant to me about Paige's enduring love for her father. Despite his criminal acts, he was a good father to Paige. Rather than give in to bitterness and rage, she chooses to care for her dying father and to honor his last wishes. In that his actions cost her so much, it speaks volumes about her character and her wide-open heart.

More times than not, I discover that my books have a common thread of forgiveness running through them. I'm always surprised by it, since I never set out to go down that path. Perhaps forgiveness lies at the root of so many of the challenges we face, whether it is forgiveness of oneself or forgiveness of another person.

I thoroughly enjoy hearing from readers. There are many ways to reach me. You can email me at scalhoune@

gmail.com or visit me at my website, bellecalhoune.com. You can also connect with me at my Author Belle Calhoune Facebook page or find me on Twitter @BelleCalhoune.

Blessings,
Belle Calhoune

A mystery writer and a shy librarian find love on a dark, stormy night in Honey Ridge, Tennessee...

BARE FEET SOUNDLESS on the cool tile flooring, Carrie moved to a pantry and removed one of Julia's sterling silver French press urns. "We'll have to grind the beans. Julia's a bit of a coffee snob."

"Won't the noise disturb the others?"

Thunder rattled the house. Carrie tilted her head toward the dark, rain-drenched window. "Will it matter?"

"Point taken. You're a lifesaver. What's your name?"

"Carrie Riley." She kept her hands busy and her eyes on the work. The fact that she was ever-so-slightly aware of the stranger with the poet's face in a womanly kind of way gave her a funny tingle. She seldom tingled, and she didn't flirt. She was no good at that kind of thing. Just ask her sisters. "Yours?"

"Hayden Winters."

"Nice to meet you, Hayden." She held up a canister of coffee beans. "Bold?"

"I can be."

She laughed, shocked to think this handsome man might actually be flirting a little. Even if she wasn't. "Bold, it is."

As she'd predicted, the storm noise covered the grinding sound and in fewer than ten minutes, the silver pot's lever was pressed and the coffee was poured. The dark, bold aroma filled the kitchen, a pleasing warmth against the rain-induced chill.

Hayden Winters offered her the first cup, a courteous gesture that made her like him, and then sipped his. "You know your way around a bold roast."

"Former Starbucks barista who loves coffee."

"A kindred spirit. I live on the stuff, especially when I'm working, which I should be doing."

She didn't want him to leave. Not because he was hot—which he was—but because she didn't want to be alone in the storm, and no one else was up. "You work at night?"

"Stormy nights are my favorite."

Which, in her book, meant he was a little off-center. "What do you do?"

He studied her for a moment and, with his expression a peculiar mix of amusement and malevolence, said quietly, matter-of-factly, "I kill people."

COMING NEXT MONTH FROM
Love Inspired®

Available March 22, 2016

ELIJAH AND THE WIDOW
Lancaster County Weddings • by Rebecca Kertz

Hiring the Lapp family men to make repairs around her farmhouse, Martha King soon develops feelings for the younger Elijah Lapp. Now it's up to the handsome entrepreneur to show the lovely widow that age is no barrier for true love.

THE FIREFIGHTER DADDY • by Margaret Daley

Suddenly a dad to his two precocious nieces, firefighter Liam McGregory enlists hairdresser Sarah Blackburn for help. He's quickly head over heels for the caring beauty, but will the secret he keeps prevent them from becoming a family?

COMING HOME TO TEXAS
Blue Thorn Ranch • by Allie Pleiter

Returning to her childhood ranch, Ellie Buckton teams up with deputy sheriff Nash Larson to teach after-school classes to the town's troubled teens. Can she put her failed engagement in the past and find a future with the charming lawman?

HER SMALL-TOWN ROMANCE • by Jill Kemerer

Jade Emerson grew up believing Lake Endwell, Michigan, was a place where dreams come true. So why is Bryan Sheffield leaving? Can she convince the rugged bachelor to give his hometown—and love—a second chance?

FALLING FOR THE MILLIONAIRE
Village of Hope • by Merrillee Whren

When Hudson Conrick's construction company works on the women's shelter expansion at the Village of Hope, he'll prove to ministry director Melody Hammond that he's more than just an adventure-loving millionaire—he's her perfect match.

THE NANNY'S SECRET CHILD
Home to Dover • by Lorraine Beatty

Widower Gil Montgomery is clueless on how to connect with his adopted daughter—until he hires nanny Julie Bishop. He quickly notices she has a special way of reaching his little girl—and of claiming his heart.

LOOK FOR THESE AND OTHER LOVE INSPIRED BOOKS WHEREVER BOOKS ARE SOLD, INCLUDING MOST BOOKSTORES, SUPERMARKETS, DISCOUNT STORES AND DRUGSTORES.

LICNM0316

REQUEST YOUR FREE BOOKS!

2 FREE INSPIRATIONAL NOVELS
PLUS 2 FREE MYSTERY GIFTS

Love Inspired®

LII5